The Moon Warriors

A Novella

Kayla Frederick

This is a work of fiction. All of the characters and events portrayed in this novel are either products of the author's imagination or are used fictitiously.

The Moon Warriors

Cover by Amy AQ Design
Edited by Raven Heidrich

First Edition January 2024
Library of Congress Control Number: 2018910798
ISBN: 978-1-950530-90-8

1.

I LOVE THE serenity of the pumpkin patch at night. It's so quiet, I can nearly hear my heart beating. It's as if time is suspended, meaningless, and I like that I'm disconnected from the world around me. During the day, this place is packed full of people—parents with tiny children and couples out for a romantic autumn stroll—but at night, it's abandoned, and in the nothingness, I find peace. It helps, in a way, that the city cemetery is nearby—just a short walk through a strip of woods.

There are urban legends about ghosts of course, but the only one who haunts these grounds is me. I'm *drawn* to this land for reasons that at one time had been inexplicable. I understand them now, all too well. The orange leaves crunch beneath my combat boots as I walk through the entrance of the black gate. Today's a cemetery day. I trudge up the path in the grass created by nothing more than the constant travel of hundreds of pairs of feet, letting the moonlight bathe my face.

The moon is full and bright, beckoning me onward, and I listen like an obedient child. The crystal around my neck warms at the contact and begins to glow as I unclasp it, removing it from its safe place around my neck. I nestle it into the hollow of a grave at the rise of the hill, sure that it's in the best possible place to gather moonlight.

The more my crystal absorbs, the better off I'll be in the long run. I sit and wait, feeling the grass tickling my bare legs beneath the hem of my dress as I read the name on the tombstone that I've chosen to use tonight. My heart clenches in the way that it does when something *really* stings deep down to my soul. I had known the person who is buried here once, when he had been alive.

Ian Morris.

He had been my friend, my confidant, my lover, my *everything*. And now he's gone. Just a haze of memories and blurry reminders clinging on. Tears dot my eyes as I stare up at the night sky, trying to identify constellations, and take my mind off of the pain that's always lurking right beneath the surface of my mind.

Ian should be here with me, charging our crystals in the moonlight and living amongst the dead, but because of *them* he never will be again…or so they think. My skin flushes with anger as I scoop my crystals up and stuff them into my pocket. The biggest, an amethyst which had been flattened out into a ten-pointed star, hangs back in its place around my neck.

As soon as the crystal touches my skin, it flashes with color and I *feel* its power right down to every blood cell in my veins. I flex my fingers, open and closed, just feeling the tingle of power in my skin. It's the sensation that anything is possible, that I can *do* anything, that motivates me at this point. Even though I'm still near Ian's tombstone, I no longer think of him.

I'm a warrior on a mission.

I give a parting glance to the mount at my feet, whisper a prayer for my dearly departed and a prayer to keep him safe, and leave the cemetery.

In my community, there are two things that are frowned on—the craft being used for vengeance or for dark matters. With the deepest apologies to my Coven, I will break both of the golden rules tonight or I will die trying.

2.

THE BOUNDARIES BETWEEN our Coven's land and *their* hunting grounds had been established centuries ago by a group of witches and demons who wanted nothing more than to finally end their feud.

The story, as I have come to understand it, says that at one time witches and demons worked together side by side with one goal in mind—cleaning the human population of its less than savory members. Witches would use their magic to try and change a person's ways but if that wasn't enough, the demons would simply do away with them. It was simple and for a long time, it worked, but for every simplicity in the world comes things to complicate it.

There were demons and witches who did not follow through with the job that had been trusted to them. Everyone is a pawn to their own devices. Those things which lift us up can also take us over. I have heard many variations of the story of how things crumbled away to war and chaos but the most popular is that there were witches who turned to black magic and demons who let prisoners go just for the satisfaction of watching them commit chaos in the world.

And with just a few bad souls in the mix, all trust was lost on both sides.

That's how the split between us and them began. For as long as the war raged on, neither side came out victorious. For centuries witches and demons slayed one another with no one coming out better for it. Finally, they had had enough and wished for nothing more than peace. The boundaries had been the solution they had finally come to. Them over there and us over here. Forever.

Until Ian's death.

The other witches in my Coven—the Moon Warriors, as they like to call themselves— don't believe the demons to be responsible for what happened. Our lifestyles are dangerous. *Everything* is dangerous. Especially the humans. When news first reached me about his untimely demise, I had assumed it was one such beast who had taken away my beloved.

After all, Ian was young and healthy, but when I saw his body, I knew the truth. See there was something about him that the other Moon Warriors didn't know—he had a habit of dabbling in black magic. At first, it was nothing too serious, just a curse here or there but curiosity is a double-edged blade and even though it may help you to wield it, it can hurt you on the backswing.

The materials for his projects weren't cheap, or easy to obtain.

Obtaining them meant doing the one thing we had vowed to never do—cross the boundary. It meant consorting with *them*, befriending them. My heart hurts at the thought. I had known about his habits, known about everything he was doing, but instead of stepping in, of stopping him before something could happen, I turned a blind eye.

For some reason, I *trusted* them to care for him, to consider him as one of their own and look after him. But they hadn't. They had murdered him in cold blood and tonight, I'm determined to find out why. Not to mention kill whoever, or *whatever*, was responsible.

I cross through the woods with that at the forefront of my mind. In the back of my mind, however, I can hear a faint attempt to contact me by Abigail, my closest friend in the Coven. I can't let her in on what I'm about to do. IF she talks to me, she has the power to calm me. If I lose my anger, I won't have the nerve left to do this, to do *any* of it.

I suck in a breath and finally come to it—the boundary between our land and theirs. It's not a physical distinction, just a creek in the woods to those who don't know, but I *do* know and my heart beats erratically as I toss stones into the water to cross over the imaginary but oh-so-real boundary line.

I step down carefully, hunching down as if I expect alarms to go off the second I come into contact with the ground on this side but nothing happens. The woods are just as cold and unreliable as they had been on my side of the boundary line so I push onward, into the dead of night.

I don't know much about what I'll find on this side. Nearly nothing at all about what to expect. For all of my questions, Ian would never tell me a thing about his travels. I know why. He thought he was protecting me. The less I know, the better, right?

Wrong.

This is going to be hard. With no information on the proper way to proceed, this could become very dangerous, very fast. And yet I feel no fear. If Ian could walk these paths with ease, then I can do the same. The crystal around my neck only seems to grow brighter as I move and I know that's partly because it's feeding off my emotions, taking away every negative thing that I *should* be feeling.

Abigail makes an attempt to contact me again, but the connection is even weaker on this side and I hope she doesn't already know what I'm doing. If anyone could take a guess about my crazy side, it's her.

I pull my shawl tighter around my shoulders even though the heat of Indian summer brings beads of sweat to my temples. I don't want to be seen before I'm ready for a confrontation, before I'm prepared on what I'm going to do. My best chance of survival, and success, depends on staying hidden for as long as possible, scoping out not only the land in case I need to make a quick escape, but to also delve as much information from whatever I see as possible.

When the trees come to an end, I'm surprised to see that the city on the other side is very much like our own. The houses and buildings are beautiful though structurally I'd guess they're a few centuries old. *Built before the war?* I muse. We have nothing left from that time, our land taking the worst of the damage from the war. Many of our buildings are less than a few decades old. It's like our town is always under construction, the work never quite complete.

As I gaze around, I have just a moment where my brain contradicts itself. My entire life, I've been told of the demons' savagery, of their brutality being so severe that they couldn't even be around one another for fear of getting into a fight. The town before me says otherwise. If I didn't know differently, I never would've guessed this place was filled with demons. It looks no different from my home town, from my Coven's town, and now I know I'm really in danger my curiosity is piqued.

I move onward into the shadows, walking seamlessly along the sidewalk of the nearest road as if it's a road I've walked my entire life. I pass a bakery, a post office, and a clothing store and once again, I'm at a loss for words. *They enjoy the pleasures of humanity too.*

With that thought in my mind, I'm not surprised when the street ends in a bar. There are cars outside and even on the street, I swear I can hear conversations going on inside. It makes sense that they would crowd as many as possible inside.

Based on what I've seen, I've come to the conclusion that the demons won't make their darkness obvious. Maybe there are humans who live here too but whatever the case, the demons won't have a shop labeled "Supplies for Black Magic."

That information is more of a need-to-know basis, Ian had said once. I thought it had been a sarcastic way of him avoiding telling me the truth but now, it might have a double meaning. The seller is most likely underground.

If that's the truth, what better, more cliché place to begin looking than somewhere like the sleazy bar before me? I force myself onward before my internal dilemma decides to take me in another direction. There are two demons by the entrance, girls whispering to one another, but neither of them look my way as I pass into the bar.

The hood of my cloak is still up over my head, concealing my hair and most importantly, my eyes. That's the difference between them and us. While their eyes are endless pits of blackness, our shine with the same color as our chosen crystal. For me, that means purple just like the amethyst around my throat. Until they see my eyes, they'll know no different.

I take a seat at the bar, hood pulled low to shadow my face, and try to observe the scene around me without looking at anyone directly. The bar is *full,* so full that it's almost impossible to find a seat anywhere. Music blasts from the speakers in the ceiling. A few demons dance but other than that, they're huddled at the tables, in the booths, at the bar just talking away.

I wonder what things demons have to talk about. With the thought of their average looking village, I have to suppress a giggle at the idea of them fretting about minimum wage jobs and clothing stores.

Then a voice says, "You don't belong here," and my blood runs cold.

3.

I DON'T TURN to look at him. Instead, he shoos away the girl who had been seated in the stool beside me and sits on it. He drums his fingers on the bar for a long moment and I'm sure he can see the tension in my shoulders and my ramrod straight spine. Why isn't he talking? And for that matter, why haven't I run yet? I stare at his fingers, the sound like a metronome controlling my panic, and contemplate my options. My identity has been compromised and it hasn't even been five minutes since I entered. I glance around the bar but no one else seems to have taken notice of me. If what I am is obvious, they don't care. Should I run while I still have the chance or leave my fate in the hands of this *demon*?

I am very much like a stray, the wild ones who duck down when you approach, hoping to not be seen, to let my existence go without passer-bys being any the wiser. When someone sees through my guard, I don't know what to do and I duck down, assuming that detection means death, but I know what my gut tells me to do—run away like an alley cat with its tail between its legs.

"Barkeep," the demon says, his deep raspy voice perfectly calm as if we're not both aware of the fact that we are mortal enemies and I've broken the treaty between us by just being here. "Whiskey on the rocks for me and my date."

I still at the words but don't say anything as the bartender readies the drinks and approaches with them, placing one in front of the demon then one in front of me. He stops for a moment as the glass clinks against the bar, and for a heart stopping second, I wonder if he knows the truth as well.

Finally, he turns away to get a drink for another demon. The demon beside me smiles down at the cup in his hand before he swirls it subtly and takes a large sip of his whiskey.

"Your date?" I ask at last, turning slightly toward him but not enough for him to see much of my face.

"Would you rather me say the truth?" he asks, sideways smile on his face as he sets the cup back to the bar.

I say nothing.

His eyes move to the untouched glass before me. "Drink," he orders.

"I don't drink," I say, also staring at the frosty glass before me. The last thing I trust is a drink from a demon. He could've signaled the bartender to put *anything* in it and I'd be none the wiser.

The demon raises his eyebrows as if he thinks I'm insane, and maybe he does, he knows? He finishes off the rest of his drink with a strong gulp before he sets his completely empty cup on the bar and clicks his tongue. "Now, I think I've done my charity work for the day. You owe me answers."

Now I raise *my* eyebrows. I have heard stories of demon arrogance but it still surprises me just the same. "Do I?"

"If you plan on relying for me as your cover," he replies coolly. "Otherwise, I can simply call you on what you are and throw you to the wolves."

"You wouldn't," I say but my heart is already beating with the anticipation that he *can* and he *will*.

"What are you doing here?" he asks flatly and glances over his shoulder to make sure no one is paying attention to our conversation.

I do the same, but the demons seem engrossed in their own activities which leaves me to wonder why the one beside me is suddenly on edge. I sigh and let my gaze drop back to the glass on the counter. "I'm looking for someone," I say at last.

"You're a long way from home, Dorothy," he sneers and picks up my glass to drain the amber liquid inside as well.

"Not necessarily. Black magic is always just around the corner, isn't it? Even when you least expect it."

The corner of his mouth pulls up. "So many witches turning to the dark side. What are they doing to you on that side of the border, I wonder."

On reflex, I turn and look him full in the face for the first time. His black eyes stare back at me from his handsome sculpted face and only too late do I look away again. If there's one thing my Coven has been careful to tell me is to *never* look into the eyes of a demon.

Especially when you're in a dangerous situation.

He looks back and by the expression on his face I can tell that he really *sees* me, both inside and out, and the look scares me. Despite my multiple layers of clothing, I feel naked and exposed as if he can see every fear, doubt, and weakness in my mind.

"The guy I can understand but you? You look like you could be a goddess," he says at last and slams the second glass onto the bar.

I'm not sure which of the comments hits me harder.

"You've seen a…male witch in here?"

The demons lets out a little scoff of a laugh. "Sure did."

"What did he look like?" I ask, heart pounding.

Is it possible that *this* demon is the one who killed Ian? Seems too simple for me to have found him so easily but who knows? Maybe the Gods are working in my favor for once.

"I can't tell you that right now. It's dangerous to talk here," he says, glancing over his shoulder yet again. "There are too many eyes and ears."

I narrow my eyes but manage to avoid looking at him this time. "I'm not leaving with you."

"Surely you're not all looks and no brain?" he asks.

"I'm smart enough to know that it's *never* a good idea to go somewhere with a demon."

Then I feel a tap on my shoulder on the *opposite* side from the demon I'm currently talking to. "Excuse me, Miss," the voice says, smooth as honey.

I tense but don't look at him. My eyes stay on the bar and I reach for the empty glass beside me without making it obvious. The demon beside me shifts, sitting higher to glare at the demon over the top of my head. Before anyone says another word, I feel cold fingers grasp into my hood and rip it off my head, exposing my curly black hair and purple eyes for everyone here to see.

"You're not welcome here, *witch*!" the demon behind me hisses and lunges forward as if he's planning to hit me in the face.

I'm prepared for it. The glass is light in my hand, and it

shatters easily when it makes contact with his face. Blood and glass rain to the floor and he screams in agony, lifting his hands to desperately try and remove the stubborn shards. The demon who had been sitting beside me pulls me away from him as every head in the bar turns in our direction. There's not a single friendly face among the group as they converge, all of them glaring at me. The demon who had been sitting beside me doesn't seem fazed by how grossly outnumbered we really are. He grabs a pool cue from a nearby table and cracks it over the head of a different demon who attempts to throw a punch at me.

A girl lunges for us but we dodge and her fists land on a different girl behind us and then Hell is born. No longer are the demons just going after us, they're hitting each other with such force that it's hard to believe they're not breaking bones. I back away from the thickest part of the fight, looking for the easiest escape route when the "friendly" demon from before grabs my arm and looks me in the eye.

"Ready to go now?" he asks.

Every instinct to argue has been wiped clean by the dozens of unfriendly eyes in the bar. I don't know why he's helping me, but he seems to be the only one who will. I don't argue as he pulls me outside into the night, leaving the bar full of angry, blood-thirsty demons brawling it out behind.

4.

WE RUN AND run and run. Blocks, streets, *miles*, and he doesn't seem any worse for the wear. I'm panting, heart pounding, the edges of my vision are starting to blacken giving me one of the worst cases of tunnel-vision I've ever had. I swoon over my feet and finally, the demon stops running, ducking into the cover of a nearby alley. I gladly take the opportunity to sit down beside a dumpster and I look up at him through the shadows.

He doesn't look at me, his gaze focused out toward the street as if he's ready to knock out every demon that's decided to follow us this far. His face looks just the same now as it had in the bar even for the fight and the long sprint that had happened in between.

"Looks as if we're in the clear now, witchy," he says, black eyes finally finding me in the shadows.

"Why did…you save me?" I ask, panting for breath as I hold a hand to my side, pushing away the pain that's throbbing there.

The demon sets his fingers to the wall, glancing out into the street again before looking back at me. "I don't know. It just seems like you have a great story to tell and I'm a sucker for a good tale."

"I don't even know your name," I say.

"I'll show you mine if you show me yours," he says with a wink.

I glare up at him, still trying to get my head to stop

swimming. The last thing I want is to pass out.

He holds his palms up. "Alright, alright. Don't look at me like that. It was just a joke. I'm Marcus."

I stare at him. Such a normal name for a supposed monster.

He stares back, widening his eyes a bit. "This is the part where you tell me yours…?"

"Talia," I say, finally finding the strength to stand to my feet. I lean heavily against the wall, testing out my legs to make sure the worst of the cramps have all but disappeared.

He bobs his head in approval. "Not a bad name at all, my dear." Then he freezes and glances back out at the street, taking just one small step backward to conceal himself completely in the lip of shadows at the entrance of the alley.

"What is it?" I ask, eyes wide as I try to disconnect myself from the wall.

"We're not safe yet."

"Where do we go?" I ask, staring down the alley though all I can see is blackness the further on it goes. The *thought* of more running leaves me ready to collapse. I don't know how much more I can take before my body will simply give out on me.

"Not far now," Marcus assures, rushing past me down the alley and I follow him, knowing I have no other choice.

I would be no match for the crowd if it caught up to me here. Even if somehow, I was, we've run so far into the depths of demon territory that I don't know how to get back to my Coven from here. After the incident in the bar, I have no doubt that the entire town will be searching for me. It doesn't help that nearly *all* of my features are distinctive. If Marcus decides he's tired of me, then I'm in some real trouble.

Can't think about that now! Then I pause, considering. *Abigail, can you hear me?*

No response. Not that I expected there to be after I cut off communication earlier. Marcus comes to a stop at the end of the alley where a patch of mud and muck has been sloshed against the bricks on the wall.

"We're here," he says, tapping his finger to the dirty rocks.

"It's a dead end," I say pointedly.

"Maybe to you witches," he says and pokes me in the nose before he sets his other hand to the grimy wall.

I scrunch my face, knowing he couldn't *pay* me to touch that wall, and watch as the "mud" on the wall begins to change colors under his hand. It lightens to a purple similar to my eyes before it rises up, the bricks disappearing beneath the muck, and a light appears, a sliver of brightness before it disappears all at once and a door stands in place. I stare at it dumbfounded, unsure of what I just witnessed.

Marcus removes his hand from the wall and grasps the knob, pulling it open to reveal darkness on the other side before he looks at me and smiles. "After you, m'lady."

Not a phrase I've ever wanted to hear from a demon, really, but when I glance between the darkness of the pit and Marcus' calm face, I know that I don't have any other choice. A drunk demon is better than no ally at all. He proved that much in the bar.

Without him, I'd most likely be tied to a stake and burned right now.

Like I'm about to dive into a pool of water, I hold my breath and rush into the darkness, not sure what to expect on the other side. Marcus follows behind me, his laughter following me as he closes the door, submerging us momentarily in darkness.

"I can't see."

"Hold on," Marcus says and I hear the tug of a pullcord before a single bare lightbulb fills the room.

I look around—expecting what, I don't know—but I'm surprised when I don't see it. The place we're in is simple, a small room with a sofa and a table. There's a window on the wall opposite from the door but it's been sealed in with bricks. Past the "window" is a dark hallway that I'm not curious at all to see where it goes. I turn to Marcus as he plops down on a sofa, slinging his jacket across the back before he stares at me expectantly to do the same.

"Where are we?" I ask as my eyes finally come to a rest on him.

He laughs. "What charming naivety! My house."

That's such a normal response in these unusual times that I shake off the insult. "Are we safe here?"

"Safer than out there," he says with a shrug.

I can't resist another glance to the brick-filled window and with that, my body cries out for rest. I sit down on the floor in the place I had been standing, feeling the instant relief in all of my screaming muscles.

Marcus raises an eyebrow and glances quizzically at the

expanse of empty sofa beside him. "Well, we're most likely going to be here for a while if we're going to wait out that crowd so I think it's story time."

I run a hand through my curly black hair, peeling off the single strands that had been plastered to my neck with sweat. "I'm not sure where to begin."

"You said at the bar that you were looking for somebody," Marcus says, sitting forward to set his hands on his knees.

I bob my head and look down at my nails, trying to decide the best way to explain from here. "Yes."

His eyes stretch wide as he waits impatiently for me to continue. "And?"

"Who was the other witch? The one dabbling in black magic?" I ask, avoiding his question.

Understanding dawns across Marcus' face. "Ah. Friend of yours, was he?"

"Possibly," I say, wondering just how much of Ian's fate Marcus actually knows. "What did he look like?"

Marcus shrugs. "At the bar, he always disguised his appearance using magic so he looked like just another demon."

I scrunch my face. "Then how do you know he was a witch?"

"He was a regular and really, that kind of disguise can't fool me. Plus, he always went by the same alias. Shadow," Marcus replies. "In my opinion, if you're going to go *that* far with magic, at least change your damn name once in a while."

Marcus' words are little more than background noise. My

heart could stop beating and I don't think I'd notice. Shadow. That was the name *I* always called Ian and I thought just me alone.

You are the light to my darkness, and I am the darkness to your light because without one, there cannot be the other, he had said.

Like an idiot, I had eaten it up without thinking twice of the possible meaning behind it. "That's him," I say stiffly.

Marcus picks up on the reaction and his eyebrows shoot up in surprise. "Doesn't seem as if you're too happy with even the thought of him. Why come all this way for a witch you hate?"

I stare at him but don't know how to answer. People do crazy things for love, it's true, but I don't want to admit that out loud. If Marcus knows about Ian's business on this side of the border then he might have known him better than I had. The thought stings and I pinch the inside of my left wrist to distract my mind from spiraling too deep while in Marcus' company.

"He was murdered," I say at last, for once not picturing the memory. "And his body was left on my doorstep."

Marcus breathes in deep as if he had expected that answer. "Look, I know what you're probably thinking but I promise I had nothing to do with that. The only time I ever saw him was at the bar. Never before and never after."

For some reason, I believe him. A cynical voice in the back of my mind tries to convince me that it's because I looked into his eyes, that he's brainwashing me like my Elders have always told me demons will do if given the chance.

But he hasn't. I know he hasn't. He wouldn't have risked everything to get me out of that bar if he was the bad guy, right?

He would've just let the others tear me apart or would've been the first to do so. I hold onto that thought, tightly and desperately, and hope that all the cynicism in the world won't make me lose that grip.

"What did he do in the bar?" I ask, voice raspy with hesitation.

"He'd get a drink or two and talk to a guy named Reddick," Marcus continues, and I fall out of my internal musings to stare at him.

"Who's that?"

"Witchy, if you're in the market to get messed up in the same things as your friend, you're not off to a good start."

"You don't say," I spit, waving my arms to showcase the situation I'm currently in.

"Well, Reddick, in my opinion, he's scum, but officially he sells supplies. Bones, plants, spellbooks, you know, all the bullshit for black magic. A lot of it is just junk really, fakes he sells to make a little extra profit."

I send him a scathing look.

"What?" he asks and shrugs. "Like I said, the guy is a scumbag. If your friend had the real stuff…well…it never comes for cheap."

"That…sounds about right," I admit and hang my head. I don't know what about his tone that leaves me feeling ashamed, but it does.

Marcus grins. "You *knew*? What kind of spells were you in the market for?"

"I'm not…" I swallow and trail off.

"What? Cat got your tongue?" he jeers. "What is it with you witches coming to the dark side?"

I look at him but don't speak right away. "I don't know. I'm not here for supplies, or black magic, or anything that Ia— *Shadow*—got himself into. I'm just…"

"Here for answers?" he guesses.

I nod, glad that I won't have to explain much more than I already have because really, I don't think I have it in me to do so. "Do you know Reddick?"

"Not personally," Marcus replies. "I've seen him around and I know what he does but for the most part, I've kept our conversations limited."

"Oh," I reply, "But you know how to get in touch with him?"

Marcus sighs and sits forward, resting his elbows on his knees. "Maybe but with the bar knocked out, I'll have to think of another way to approach him."

5.

THERE'S UNCOMFORTABLE SILENCE in the house for a time period that lasts too long for my comfort. So, I get up, skirting the edges of the room and looking at everything the place has to offer.

"We're in for a long night," Marcus admits, watching me from his place on the sofa. "Do you want something to eat? I don't have much but maybe we could go out and grab a bite while we figure this out? Maybe get a coffee? Caffeine could do you some good."

I rub at my eyes, feeling the bags that must be obvious at this point. I can't remember the last time I've slept and while caffeine does sound like Heaven, I wonder if it'll really be able to help me in this state. After all, caffeine does not cure existential exhaustion.

"How can we go anywhere? Won't they be looking for us? For *me*?" I ask, turning to look at him.

Marcus considers it, staring at me for the longest moment. "I doubt it. They've probably already forgotten all about it and gone back to drinking and whatever the hell else it is they do."

I stare at him, drawing my eyebrows together. Somehow, I doubt it could be that easy. "I'm a *witch*," I remind him.

Marcus shrugs. "And? The treaty has never been as big of a deal to us as it is to your kind."

That explains their less than apparent concern for Ian's trips.

"Okay," I sigh and my shoulders slump.

Who am I to argue with him? For a demon, he has extended more kindness to me than I thought they were even capable of and I'm still not really sure why. Is it possible that the stories of them enjoying fighting are so true that they'll swoop on *any* opportunity they get to do so? I lift my hand to press at my temple feeling in no mood to try and figure it out.

I've got enough other problems on my plate and if I'm going to get to the bottom of Ian's mystery, I need to forget everything else. Despite Marcus' assurances that the other demons will have lost interest, I'm uneasy as we leave his house. He leads the way without being asked to do so, keeping me cloaked in his own shadow as we travel across town. I'm constantly searching over my shoulder, convinced there will be demons *waiting* for us, but no one says a word as we approach a diner that looks abandoned from the parking lot. I pull my hood back up over my head as we approach the door. Inside it's calm and quiet, reminding me of a scene straight out of the '50's. Marcus leads us to a booth in the back and insists I sit nestled against the wall with him on the other side of me.

He must think I'm a fool if I don't recognize the signs for what they are—he's worried which means we aren't out of the clear just yet. Marcus doesn't say anything about it, pretending that it's just a typical day. He orders two plates of food and when he sets mine in front of me, I just stare at it.

He's already wolfed half of his own portion down before he even notices my hesitation. "It's not poisoned," he assures me.

I don't feel any better. I peer at him from under the edge

of my hood. "How can you be so sure?"

"These are good people here."

I snort before realizing that he's serious. That's a hard thought for me to accept. Demons? Being *good*? He blinks at me, looking fairly insulted until I pick up my fork and stuff a bite into my mouth. Marcus bobs his head approvingly and puts the last bite of his food in his mouth.

The pancakes are warm and moist, and my stomach accepts the offering with a greedy growl. Not only has it been a while since I've slept, I can't remember my last meal. I take another bite, encouraged by the fact that Marcus got through his portion without complaint and he looks even happier for it. Marcus stops chewing abruptly, eyes caught on something across the café before he stands up, pushing away his empty dishes with a clatter. I stop, mid-bite as if someone had pressed the pause button on me.

"I'll be right back," he says without further explanation and hurries away before I even have the time to set the fork down.

In that moment, I find myself questioning every life choice that I've ever made that's led me to this point in time. I feel stupid, sitting in the booth alone, surrounded by my worst enemy, *eating* the food they've given me. I don't know where Marcus is going and as such, I don't know if he'll come back. What if the riot from the bar finds me here before he returns?

My anxiety eases when he reappears less than a minute later but when I see that he's not alone, I want to throw up everything I had just eaten.

6.

I MUST LOOK as feral as I feel because Marcus holds his hands out, a peace sign to both me and his companion who is staring at me with the same expression I imagine myself to be using while staring right back at him.

"It's okay, everybody's fine," Marcus says, sliding back into his seat beside me. "This is Talia. Talia, this is my friend, Alec."

The word "friend" should ease away any uncertainty I feel but it doesn't. Alec is a big hulking thing with short brown curls and a face that looks battle ready. He slips into the seat across from me and we take a long moment just to stare at one another.

"You'll pardon my friend for staring. He's never seen a female witch before," Marcus whispers in my ear.

Alec frowns at him. "Not true. I'm just not *used* to seeing them, that's all."

Marcus laughs and sits back in his seat. "Tomato, tamato, really."

"Does he know Reddick?" I ask and the good cheer disappears from Alec's face immediately.

"She knows Reddick?" he asks Marcus. "How does she know Reddick?"

The panic on his face should concern me but it doesn't. All I'm focused on is the fact that he *knows* this mystery demon, the one I need to track down in order to figure out what happened to Ian the final time he crossed the boundary.

"How do *you* know Reddick?" I retort, catching and holding his eyes despite every cautionary tale I've ever heard in my life.

"I-I…" he flounders for words and I realize that despite his exterior, this is not a tough man, not a fighter. He's sensitive and pinned under my stare, he's panicking. That tickles me in the same way Marcus' words had when he said "good people."

"He works for Reddick," Marcus says at last.

I whirl on him. "He *works* for him? What does that mean?"

"Relax. Nothing bad. He's an errand boy."

Alec lets out an offended "hmmph." "I'm worth more than that."

Marcus waves his hand in a gesture meant for Alec to explain himself.

Alec give him a scathing glance before dips a bit closer, eyes locked on mine. "Okay, I *do* work for him but it's…not like I'm into black magic myself. I gather things for him. Supplies."

"You're a dealer then?" I ask and Marcus bursts into laughter.

"In a way, I suppose," Alec says, taking no notice of Marcus' background noise. "He puts in requests. I gather the supplies and he pays me. No questions, no answers."

"So, hypothetically, you could lead me to him then."

Alec furrows his brow, eyes shifting between me and Marcus as if he's not sure how to answer that. "You're serious? He'll tear you up and throw you out with today's trash! Why in the world would you want to get into contact with *Reddick*?"

"Not for whatever reason you're probably assuming," I assure him. "I'm…" I swallow, again unsure of how much information to divulge.

"She's looking for information about her friend," Marcus says, deciding for me.

"You have friends on this side of the border?" Alec asks, raising an eyebrow. "I feel as if I would've seen you around before now if that's accurate. These are small circles after all."

I drop my gaze to the table and for anyone passing by, it probably looks as if I'm glaring at my unfinished plate of food. Despite the fact that I'm here for Ian, I suddenly feel ashamed to talk about it as if whatever he's done somehow reflects negatively on myself. And maybe it does.

"Had. *Had* a friend on this side of the border. He…dabbled in things he shouldn't have and got himself into trouble."

"Ah," Alec says, face smoothing into calm clarity that makes me feel even worse than his curiosity had. "A witch."

I bob my head. "Shadow, did you know him?"

Alec freezes instantly. "The name…is familiar."

My heart pounds painfully in my chest but I can't determine what emotion stirs the reaction. "I can't really describe him to you." I pause to sigh. "Apparently, he used magic to change his appearance every time he crossed the border. The name…the name is all I have to go on." I can feel the stinging in the back of my eyes again and I blink furiously to make it go away.

I will not cry.

"If he was close to Reddick, I'm good without knowing

all the details," he assures me, reaching across the table to touch my hand gently.

I tense, assuming it will burn but nothing happens, and I stare at my hand in amazement when he pulls his away. The shock, as it turns out, is an excellent distraction from my sorrow.

"So, will you lead us to Reddick or not?" Marcus asks.

I cut my eyes at him, holding up a hand to stop Alec before he can reply. "Hold on. *We?*"

Marcus nods, cocking his head as if he's offended by the question. "I think I'm just as invested in this whole thing as you at this point."

I stare at him, once again not understanding why he bothered to involve himself in the first place. If the situation had been reversed, I most likely would've never intervened, letting fate do what it would. I guess that's the difference between him and me.

"Fine," I say grudgingly and turn back to Alec. "Can you take *us* to him, please?"

Alec taps his fingers on the table for a long moment, looking thoughtful. "I can if you make me just one promise."

"Shoot," Marcus says, and I barely repress the urge to glare at him again. *I* should be the one making bargains, not him. I sigh and the anger leaves. I guess in a way it's fair. Without him, I probably wouldn't have even gotten this far. I should be grateful for all he's done and even more grateful that he's still here. I can't bring myself to pull out that emotion so I suppose the least I can do is let him call the shots.

"Don't say a word to Reddick about me."

Marcus grins and holds his massive hand out across the table. "Deal, brother."

7.

WHILE THE REST of the town might be higher than my expectations, Reddick's building is exactly how I pictured a demon's hangout would be. It's shadowy, so dense around the building that in the dead of night, I can't tell what it looks like. I have a chill down my spine that tells me it's probably for the best that I can't see it. If I could, I would most likely turn around and abandon my mission on the spot.

Alec points us to the entrance on the side of the building but before we can get clarification on the story we're supposed to tell, he's slipped away into the very shadows that we just came through.

I look up at Marcus and he looks back at me. "Ready for this?" he asks, face crafted in deadly concern.

"Is there really such a thing?" I grumble and pull my cloak tighter around my shoulders as I hustle forward.

Marcus sets a hand on my shoulder and I realize it's to slow me. He keeps his pace at my side, glancing left and right as if he expects us to be ambushed at any moment. The more I watch him, the more it sinks in that this really is a dangerous situation. Not just for me. He's risking a lot for me and I don't even have the decency to repay him by looking over my own damn shoulder.

Pride is a sin for a reason, I scold myself and that somehow makes my mood even worse.

Marcus smirks as he bangs on the door and I cringe, the sound ringing out into the silence of the night making it even louder than it probably is.

"Relax. You're acting like you don't belong here," Marcus says to me as we wait for some response on the other side of the door.

I scoff and reach up to knock this time. "That's because I *don't*."

"Maybe not but you don't want him to know that."

"He'll know when he *sees* me," I point out, gesturing to my face.

"He might be able to figure out where you're from but that doesn't mean shit about how he'll see *you* as a person…witch…whatever the fuck you are. Unlike your Elders, these demons don't give a damn about the treaty."

"Fair enough," I say and bang on the door one more time just as it swings open.

I can't see the demon on the other side of the door but by the outline of the shadow, I can tell he's a large being, cloaked in black everywhere from his hands to his feet. The only part of him that I can actually see is the bit of his face that's exposed beneath the brim of his hood.

Somehow, that little bit of exposure makes him even more terrifying because I can only *guess* what the rest of him looks like. Even though I've got my hood hanging low as well, I doubt I come across even half as frightening as he does.

"Yes?" he asks voice loud and commanding but at the same time devoid of emotion, of *humanity*.

"I'm looking for Reddick," I say instantly.

The figure is quiet, *staring* at me before the bit of exposed face turns to Marcus. I know what he's thinking without him saying a word. A witch and a demon? It confuses even him. "We don't serve your kind here," he says to me at last and goes to close the door.

That changes something in me. "The Hell you don't!" I snarl and lash out, putting my boot in the way before the wood can slam shut.

He struggles to close it anyway and I can feel the heavy surface grinding the bones in my foot, but I push in the opposite direction, forcing it open the best I can. Marcus is frozen beside me, unsure which side of the fight he should take, but when I glance up at him with the demand for help in my eyes, he joins in and less than a minute later, the door is flung open with us on the threshold.

Reddick takes a step backward but his lips curve into a smile. "For a lowly witch, you're brave."

"Hell hath no fury like a woman scorned," I retort and glance to Marcus.

He fights back a laugh, forcing his face to take on something that resembles grim determination.

"And what stops me from having you both killed right here, right now?" he sneers.

Marcus doesn't look so thrilled at this point.

"Your curiosity," I say. "You're intrigued by us, our situation."

I still can't see his face but for some reason, I know that he's impressed by the answer. "Ah, very astute."

"You knew my friend," I accuse.

He holds his hands out and laugh. "My dear girl, I know

many people."

"How many of them have you killed?" I snarl.

"Easy," Marcus mutters to me, grasping my wrist suddenly as if he's afraid I'll lunge at Reddick.

If I was sure of the situation, I might do just that, but this is a situation I'm far from comfortable in. I haven't forgotten how dangerous Reddick is—the fear in Alec's eyes is hard to shake off. For all I know, Reddick is made more of shadows than a corporal body and I'd only be hurting myself and my own cause by acting so hasty.

Reddick doesn't seem offended by the insinuation. Instead he laughs and laughs, the sound rumbling the very walls and ceiling. I glance around, worried the flimsy structure will collapse but it doesn't.

"I do not hurt anyone, witch," he says at last. "I merely supply the tools and what they do from there determines their own fate. Black magic does not come without its own dangers. Whatever you do onto others comes back to you threefold."

I frown and want so desperately to argue but know that I have no grounds to do so I just stay silent.

Marcus must sense the shift in mood in me because he speaks up once again. "We're looking for a witch named Shadow."

Reddick begins to laugh, the sound seemingly coming from him and every shadowy corner of the room all at once. I glance around, subtly taking a step backward until I'm pressed against Marcus' side.

"I am...*aware* of him," Reddick says at last and the laughter subsides.

When the surprise from his outburst fades, it's replaced with anger and I charge forward, toward the darkest mass of shadows. Marcus puts a hand on my shoulder, trying to stop me but I ignore it this time, helpless to my anger.

"How could you?" I demand, swiping for him when I feel Marcus grab my hand and tug me back.

"Are you *crazy*!?" he demands, growling in my ear.

I don't take my eyes off of Reddick. He's smiling under the rim of his hood and I can tell he's enjoying the show before him. And why not? I know what I look like—for a master of black magic, I would never be intimidating despite my best attempts.

"Oh, my. It seems you have the wrong idea about me," he says, tipping his head to the side.

I narrow my eyes. "No, I think the problem is that I see all too well what you are."

"And even if your assumptions were correct, what do you believe you can do about it? You think you can avenge him somehow? That you stand a chance against me?"

I reach up to grasp the glowing pendant around my throat and the smile on Reddick's face only intensifies. He reaches into his pocket and pulls out the tiniest skull I've ever seen. A rat skull, I assume by the shape. He makes sure that both Marcus and I see it then he closes his hand into a fist, reducing the tiny bone to dust. Instantly, the light in my crystal goes out and a pain radiates through my chest. I gasp and take a stumbling step forward, hand clutching at my skin as my knees buckle beneath me.

I collapse to the floor, unable to breathe and desperately trying to figure out a way how. Marcus drops to the floor beside me. I feel his hand on my hip but other than that, my vision is becoming a pinpoint, the edges as dark as the shadows in Reddick's body.

"What are you doing to her?" Marcus demands.

I risk one glance back up at Reddick before the room around me turns black.

8.

WHEN I COME back to consciousness again, I feel as if I'm floating on a cloud. My body feels weightless and I reach out through the darkness, but I can't see anything. I don't know where I am, but there's a voice in the back of my head that reminds me I should be concerned.

Bit by bit my memory returns to me and then the room around me comes to focus. My vision is still just a pinpoint when I open my eyes, but it quickly opens to my full vision. The ceiling above me isn't one I recognize but when I sit up, I realize I'm on a bed which is also unfamiliar.

"Don't move too much," Marcus' voice floats into my mind.

When I turn in the direction of the sound, I see that he's seated on the edge of the bed beside me. He sets his hand to my forehead and I just stare at him, at the *concern* I see in his eyes. It makes no sense. I'm a stranger to him just as he is to me. We're supposed to be *enemies* and yet here he is with me…wherever *here* is.

"What happened?" I ask, licking my dry lips, and he finally pulls his hand back.

"Your bravery…does not do you any favors on this side of the boundary," he says with a great deal of restraint.

Then I remember. The skull and the black out. Reddick's laughter. Marcus' screams. "Reddick! Where he is?"

"I think it's best we don't talk about him," Marcus says, hand clenching into a fist on his lap.

"Wh-but he knows what happened to Shadow," I say quietly.

"Yeah," Marcus says, and his voice is bitter. "But you should be more concerned about what happened to yourself."

My eyes stretch wide at the sound of venom in his voice. It's an unexpected contrast to the concern that's still so visible in the depths of his eyes. I catch his gaze for just a second, but he turns his face away and stands up so fast that the bed shifts without his weight.

"What's wrong?" I ask, reaching a hand toward him.

He doesn't turn to face me. "What's wrong?" he asks so softly and then louder, "What's wrong?"

I swallow.

He says nothing, merely holds up his left arm. I glance over his shoulder, studying his skin from his shoulder down to his hand. Then I see it, a band of black markings twirling from the back of his hand to the inside of his arm, ending in the crook of his elbow. The lines twist and cross and I stare, unsure of what I'm seeing.

"What is that?" I ask.

"The reason you're still alive," he says and storms out of the room.

I'm stunned into silence, shocked into paralysis. There are probably a million things I should be thinking about, but in the moment, all I can see are the marks on his wrist. I've seen something like that before, haven't I?

No, he wouldn't, I think and lift my fingers, chewing subtly on my nails. When I see my arm, I realize I have the exact same marks.

9.

"WH-HAT?" I STUTTER out, holding my arm as far away from me as I can as if I think that denying it will make the marks disappear somehow.

Then, I try the opposite approach and bring my arm closer, studying the design in my skin. The lines are deep, engraved. I press at them, marring them with my fingers, but they don't fade for anything. The skin around them turns red from the effort but they remain unchanged.

What did Reddick do? I think again and look up at the door Marcus had stormed through. *I have to find him.*

I toss the blanket off of me and try to stand to my feet. The second my toes touch onto the floor, I know I've made a mistake. I topple to the ground, and I cry out, reaching down to touch my legs. The skin is cold and when I try to move them, they don't comply.

"Marcus!" I cry out.

I don't expect him to respond but once again, he defies my expectations and the door flies open to reveal him standing in the frame. When he catches sight of me on the ground, he sighs. "Didn't I tell you to stay on the bed?"

"What's going on, Marcus? What did you do for me?" I ask, holding up my arm as he crouches beside me.

He purses his lips and ruffles his hair. "I did what I had to do."

"Please don't tell me you made a deal with him."

"And what would you say if I said that was exactly what happened? What would you do if I said I traded my life for yours?"

I look down at the floor, my dark hair creating a curtain around my face. "I would tell you to take it back, that you made a mistake. To let my fate be my own. You owe me no favors, especially after everything you've already done."

"And what was the alternative? Let him kill you?" Marcus asks then drops his gaze. "You *do* realize that was the plan?"

"Yes," I answer honestly, clenching my jaw in the slightest. "It's what any demon would do, right?" *Who am I kidding, that's not limited to demons. Half the witches in my Coven would've done the same.* "He would've killed me, and you would've gone on your merry way, scot free."

Marcus smiles and the expression angers me.

"That's funny to you?" I ask, glaring up at him.

"No but your nativity is." He swipes a finger under his lip, considering this. "You really haven't been outside of your Coven much if you think he'd let me go, just like that and we'd all live happily ever after."

I quirk an eyebrow. "Why not?"

"As you said, it's just not the demon way. Especially not for someone like him. I came in with you, he most likely assumes I have other witch alliances who would come sniffing around if we disappeared. Uninvited guests are the last thing he wants."

"So, you sacrificed yourself?" I try to sit up but the

numbness in my legs causes me to fall back onto my elbows again.

Marcus tilts his head to the side. "If you're a pessimist, which at this point I assume you are, you can see it that way. I prefer to think of it as I saved both of our lives."

I sigh, the breath stirring my bangs before I peer up at him through the strands of hair. "Depends on the terms of the deal."

Marcus just stares at me for a long moment and the laughter is gone. *Everything* is gone and he's in a memory inside his head. I can tell by the unfocused look in his eyes. When they finally turn to me, he opens his mouth and closes it again as if he knows more than he's willing to say. The silence kills me. I can literally feel the suspense of the moment tearing down everything in me until I finally blurt out, "What did you promise him?"

"Nothing I can't handle," he says and stands up, shaking his shoulder as if he's hoping to remove a dozen spiders that have made their way under his shirt.

I know he's going to try and walk away again but I can't let him do that. I reach out and grasp his ankle, holding him in place. He towers above me, his frame hulking, but when he looks down and catches my eyes, he deflates the slightest bit.

"What is it?" I try again, my voice much softer this time.

"He…wants me to get some old spellbook," he says, reaching up to scratch the back of his neck. "For the library."

I tilt my head to the side. That hardly seems scary considering the source of the mission. "Really?"

Marcus nods.

"What's the spellbook?"

Marcus pulls his lips to the side and looks down at me incredulously. "You think he was going to explain much more to me than what I was told?"

I push my lips out into a pout. "How can you know if you've found it or not if you don't know what you're looking for?"

"It's an old Grimoire. Apparently, I'll "know it when I find it,'" he says, mocking Reddick's voice.

I stifle a laugh. "That's something, I guess." I drop my gaze and frown.

Marcus bends down and grasps me around the waist, lifting me to set me back onto the edge of the bed. I freeze at the contact, the spots where his hands were sending little jolts of electricity through me. He doesn't notice as he pulls his hands away.

"What is it?"

"Did he…mention Shadow?" I ask.

Marcus shakes his head but suddenly, he refuses to make eye contact. "I'm going to try and find the book as quickly as I can so you can get back to your revenge and cross the border back into Wonderland."

He stands up and turns to walk away but I don't want him to go. "You think you're just going to leave me here?" I ask.

Marcus casts a crooked smile over his shoulder. "No offense, sweetheart, but you haven't proven yourself very worthy against demons so far."

"Well, now I have a reason to try harder," I point out,

holding out my arm, and the markings, so he can see them clearly.

Marcus stops walking and rests his forehead gently against the wall. "What about your legs?" his muffled voice says.

"What are you doing?" I counter.

He glances at me over his shoulder. "I was just seeing if I'd have any better luck talking to a wall since you're just as stubborn."

I glare at him and he walks back over to me, sitting on the bed. "Seriously though." He gestures to my lower half once again.

I hold out a hand and reach down my neckline, seeking out my crystal.

"I don't know what you're doing but can I help?" He winks.

My eyes narrow as the glare turns to concentration, but I'm hardly aware of my face as my fingers work faster, more erratically. I poke at the familiar skin that's used to feeling the cold metal of the amulet but it's empty.

"It's gone," I whisper, eyes wide.

"Your amulet?" Marcus asks. "Yeah, it's uh…collateral to ensure we do the mission assigned to us."

"Our *lives* weren't enough?" I ask, mouth stretched wide in shock.

Marcus shrugs. "Apparently not."

I look down at my legs, disheartened. "What are we going to do? We can't find anything if I can't even walk."

"Your crystals hold *all* your magic?"

I bob my head. "They hold the energy for it. Without them, I…"

Marcus laughs and reaches into his pocket, pulling out the tiny array of crystals I usually keep stored in my pocket. I glance from his open palm up into his face and back down again.

"So, I have some explaining to do," he says with a sheepish smile on his face.

"And I hope it's a *very* good explanation," I reply, swiping the crystals from him.

"Well, the reason I ever approached you in the bar to begin with was well…" He reaches up to scratch his neck.

"Was?" I prompt, raising an eyebrow as he makes every attempt possible to avoid my gaze.

"To pick your pockets. That's what I do. There's a reason the demons didn't spare me when they went after you. They hate me just the same."

My eye twitches. "So, what you're saying is that over the course of the last two hours, you've gone from petty criminal to martyr?"

"Pretty good character growth, right?"

I scoff and open my hand to stare down at the gems again. "What stopped you from running off after you swiped my crystals?"

"I saw your face," he says.

I raise an eyebrow. "And just like that, you're no longer a criminal?"

Marcus holds up his marked arm. "I wouldn't go that far. Now I'm just onto bigger and better things."

"Right," I say, and Marcus reaches out a finger to push

the tiny gems around my palm.

"How does this work?" he asks.

I don't say anything. I close my eyes and clench my hand again, humming softly in the beginning of a chant. The sound grows louder, and I feel the crystals warm on my skin, but it barely lasts before their power goes out completely, and I cry out, throwing them across the room like a glittering hailstorm.

Marcus looks between them on the floor and me on the bed. I look at my hand, at the tiny burn marks they had left in my palm as he asks, "What just happened?"

"Their power's been tapped."

"You can't heal?" he guesses.

I bob my head and tuck my lip between my teeth.

"You have to stay here then," he says slowly.

"No. I don't even know where *here* is!" I say, mouth wide in horror as I glance around the shadowy room.

Marcus winces as if he doesn't want to offer an explanation. "These are Reddick's bunks for his…devotees."

I glance around but find myself not wanting to obtain anymore information than that.

"Well, whatever this place is, it doesn't matter. I'm coming with you."

"And what are you going to do if I refuse? Crawl?" He laughs.

I look him dead in the eyes and say in one deadpanned word, "Yes."

The smile drops from his face and he ruffles his black hair before he says one word back. "Fuck."

10.

"WHEN I SAW you at the bar, I thought you were crazy but this?" He groans, adjusting me in his arms as he carries me out of the building. "I guess what they say about first impressions is spot on."

I wish my legs worked just so I could feel the satisfaction of stepping on his foot.

"I know you want to get to the bottom of this and all, but I doubt me carrying you bridal style will inflict fear into the hearts of the wicked. Just sayin'."

"This isn't a permanent solution," I say scornfully and then a sound interrupts me before I can manage another word.

"Talia?" a familiar voice drifts from the shadows.

I tense. It's Abigail.

Marcus freezes instantly and both of us scan the darkness ahead, seeking out the source of the voice.

"Abby? What are you doing here?" I ask when I catch a glimpse of her crystals shining in the dark. She has an affinity for rubies which leaves an eerie red light around her neck and in her eyes.

"What's happening?" Marcus asks as Abigail detaches from the shadows.

Her rubies and her height are probably the most fearsome things about her. She is tall but she's also thin making it seem as if she could be blown over with a strong enough gust of wind. She has a baby-like face and two identical brown pigtails. In the moment, she wears the same expression as

Marcus. "Talia, are you being carried by a *demon*?"

"Name's Marcus, actually. Thanks for asking," he replies, thrusting out his chin as he tries to shoulder his walk past her.

"It's okay, Marcus. She's a friend," I inform him.

He scoffs and stops briefly to looks her up and down. "Not my first impression, but sure, whatever you say, witchy."

"What are you doing here?" Abigail asks me.

I lift my eyebrows. "I could ask you the same thing!"

"You weren't answering me. I got worried," she admits and looks down at her ruby, stroking it gently between two long, pale fingers.

"How'd you know I'd be *here*?"

She shrugs. "Lucky guess? I know how hard the full moon is on you and-and are you *hurt*?"

It's then I realize my dress has hiked up and my legs are exposed, showing off the patterns of bruises I've acquired from falling so many times.

She looks up at Marcus accusingly. "Did you do this to her? And where are you taking her anyway?"

He takes on an amused expression. "Guess I'm dangerous like you're all taught to believe. Right, witchy?"

"No, Abby. He saved me," I admit, not playing into Marcus' game.

"Hmm, interesting, interesting," Marcus says. "Now why would a monster like me do such a thing?"

Abigail makes a face at him. "Put her down."

Marcus clutches me tighter to him. "Why would I do that after what terrible things you've said about me?"

She sighs and taps her foot. "Really?"

"*Really*," Marcus says, smiling.

"Alright, I'm sorry," Abby spits. "Better?"

"Eh, not an A plus performance but that's what you get when you cast a witch," he says but finally answers her plea and sets me onto the ground.

She makes a face at him and he begins to laugh.

"Again with the insane laughter?" I ask.

"Again with the naivety?" he counters.

I glare at him.

"Not you. Your…*friend?* Here. Yeah. She doesn't get demons either."

Is that the truth though? I stare at her as she drops to her knees beside me. This side of the border is no picnic. The fact that she found me with such seeming ease on her own leaves me with the feeling that, like Ian, she hasn't been entirely honest with our Coven either.

Abby goes to work with her crystals, muttering spells and working her magic. "All better," she says a few moments later and urges me to stand. Marcus helps me to do so and I'm glad to be able to feel the dirt beneath my toes again.

Abby puts her hands on her hips and stares at me. "Do I get an answer now?"

For a moment, I'm confused. I don't remember her asking a question. She looks at Marcus and it's then that I remember that I haven't told her why I'm here. "Do you really want to know?" I ask and scuff the dirt at my feet to avoid looking at her face.

Marcus cocks an eyebrow and dips down to look at my

face. "Are you *embarrassed?* What happened to the hellbent witch on a mission at the bar?"

I cringe and look up at him. He smiles back even though Abigail is also looking at him.

"What mission? I can't believe the Coven would send you here!"

I clench my hands into fists at my sides. There's no keeping it in now. "That's the thing. They didn't."

Her eyes turn into full-blown saucers.

"No one knows," I continue.

"Correction. No *witches* know," Marcus says and smiles at me. "Hi, I'm your partner in crime here, remember?"

"What do you think you're *doing?* Do you realize how dangerous this is? These things are *savages*. No offense," she says to Marcus.

He rolls his eyes.

"You don't understand!" I blurt out and feel the familiar tingling of tears in my eyes.

"And neither do you. You weren't there that night. You have no idea what happened. It's all speculation. You could die over here and for what? A gut feeling?"

"No, I do know," I say with a glance up at Marcus.

He presses his lips into a grim line and hesitantly nods back.

"Just come home," Abigail insists, twining her hand with mine. "And we can forget about this whole thing.

"It's not as easy as that," I tell her, pulling myself away from the contact just as quickly as she formed it.

"It can be."

I shake my head and hold up my arm. "You're welcome to go home at any time but I'm seeing this through to the end."

"You'll regret it. Don't be surprised if the Elders find out about this," she assures me before whisking on her heels to disappear into the darkness she had emerged from.

11.

WE GO IN the opposite direction of Abigail, both of us heavily silent. At first, it's anger that fuels me onward, but it fades long before the silence does. I'm glad. I'm sure anything out of Marcus' mouth would've been enough to dissolve me into tears and even if I'm not as tough as I wish I were, I can still *appear* that I am.

"All this work," Marcus tsks sometime later. "You must really love that Shadow guy."

I look away, purposefully doing anything I can to not look at him. "I can't say I ever loved him."

"But you're here."

"Yeah, but it's impossible to say I love someone I never truly knew. I had no idea about anything he did on this side of the border. Now for Abigail to come here and tell me to forget it all…I feel like it's related."

Marcus sighs and stops walking. I turn to give him a questioning look. "Something wrong?"

"I lied to you, back there at Reddick's. He…told me a bit about Shadow when you were unconscious."

I turn on my heels and rush up to him, grabbing him by the collar. "Tell me!"

"A little too short for that to be real effective," he says, smiling at me as he pats my hand.

I ignore the teasing and grasp onto his shirt even tighter. "What did he *say*?"

"This mission…it's because of something Ian did."

I blink once. Twice. Three times. "And you didn't think to *tell* me?"

Marcus says nothing, but there's a glint in his eye, almost like a tear. Suddenly, I get it. He didn't want me to think of Shadow, of the mess he had gotten himself into. Instead, Marcus had wanted me to think of the way he had stepped in and saved my life when I very well could've been murdered.

"For as long as I live, I'll never be able to make this up to you," I tell him. "Everything. From the bar to this." I glance at the markings on my arm.

He smirks. "I can think of a few things you can try."

I groan but inside, I wonder just how much longer I have left to live. If we fail this mission, I may have just hours left. Marcus glances at me from the corner of his eye and I wonder if he's thought the same.

"I don't know what the guy did to get you attached to him but from everything I've gathered, he was scum."

I almost don't want to ask but I do anyway. "What else *have* you heard?"

"Nothing that will make you feel any better," he says.

For some reason, I trust that to be the truth and push no further on the topic.

"We should stop soon and rest for the night," Marcus says after a while.

That catches me off guard. "Huh? Why?"

He blinks at me. "How long did you think this trip would be?"

I stare at him, dumbfounded. I hadn't actually considered it. For some reason, I had assumed that this could be simple, easy enough to accomplish in a night, but if that was the truth, wouldn't Reddick have taken care of it himself instead of sending someone else to do it for him?

Unless he doesn't want to get his hands dirty. I purse my lips.

"I was hoping to be back home by morning," I admit.

Marcus looks down at his arm. "I don't think that's possible now."

"They'll notice I'm gone if I'm not there when the sun comes up," I say, letting out a shuddering breath.

"Won't they know anyway?" he asks.

Then I remember Abigail. I'm sure she'll wake them all up just so they *will* know. "Maybe it's best to never go back."

"Que sera, sera," Marcus says with a shrug.

I bob my head. "How long of a trip *is* this?"

"Reddick wants us to find a demon who lives out in the mountains beyond town."

I stop and turn to look at him. "*Mountains?*" I feel smaller and smaller inside at the thought of just how long this mission could actually take.

"Relax, we won't actually have to climb them," he says, holding up his hands. "Hopefully. Reddick says the guy we need frequents the woods at the mountain base."

I nod and hope that to be the truth. "I guess we should get some rest them."

Marcus smiles. "I was hoping you would say that. There's a hotel coming up in about a mile."

"A hotel?" I ask. "I don't have any money." I stare at Marcus but when I remember the pickpocketing story, I make the assumption that he doesn't either.

"It's okay, I've got it," he says, chin out and head held high.

I don't know what he's planning. I'm just glad he *has* a plan.

12.

MARCUS EVENTUALLY LEADS us to a nice inn. It's small but being that it's run by demons, it's surprisingly cozy. The desk clerk asks no questions and doesn't even look all that surprised by the idea of a witch and a demon checking into a room together.

Does this happen often? I wonder.

"They don't seem to care that I'm here," I whisper as we ascend the winding staircase to our room.

He shrugs. "Why would they?"

"Well, after the whole incident at the bar, I just thought…"

Marcus laughs. "Not everyone is violent, witchy. There are some demons who care more about their own business than other people's, believe it or not."

"Whatever the reason, I'm glad for it," I admit and rumple my hair as we hit the landing onto the next floor.

Marcus smiles but doesn't speak again until after we get to our room. It's small and I notice there's only one bed. I turn to Marcus and raise an eyebrow.

He holds his hands up defensively. "Don't look at me like that. It was the best I could do."

"You never did tell me how you got the room," I muse and cross through the tiny kitchen back to the "bedroom" part of the room.

He dips two fingers into his pocket and emerges with a thin plastic card between them. "You can thank a Mister Michael

Tanner for this room." He tosses the card onto the table beside him and I laugh.

"I never thought I'd be so relieved to be friends with a criminal before." I sink to the floor, working on untying the knots in the laces of my boots.

The smile falls off Marcus' face as he leans against the wall, watching me.

"What?" I ask.

He tucks his lip between his teeth. "Nothing."

I narrow my eyes and toss my undone shoe at him. "Don't give me that. I hate that answer."

He sighs and drops to his knees beside me. "Fine. It's just, well, Shadow doesn't seem as if he was all that innocent."

"Yeah, I've thought that," I admit, going to work on untying my other shoe while at the same time keeping my eyes from letting their tears drip free.

"You've done nothing wrong by caring about him, you know?" Marcus says.

I stare harder at my shoes, my twitching fingers shaking more and more by the second and even the easiest of knots would be impossible to undo in this condition.

"You can have the bed," Marcus says and turns away as if he knows no words will make me feel better at this point.

Maybe he sees the emotion in my hands or the fact that I won't let him see my face. "Okay," I say at last and pull myself up onto the sheets.

I watch him take off his jacket and snag one of the pillows off the bed to make a makeshift spot on the floor without a single complaint and all I can do is admire him for it.

"So, why'd you stay?' I ask finally.

"Huh?" he asks, turning to glance at me over his shoulder.

"If you just wanted to pick my pockets, why did you stay after the fact? Why did you bother to ever get involved with all those demons? With Alec and Reddick?"

He props himself up on his elbows. "Contrary to what you've been told, demons are capable of compassion, empathy, and all those other gooey things that come with having a heart because believe it or not, we have those too."

I blink and set my head back onto the pillow. My entire life my Coven has brainwashed me. Looking into Marcus' eyes, I know that now. Eventually, Marcus lays back down as well, but I can't stop staring at the back of his head, remembering his words.

History is taught in a way that leaves the receiver of the information impressionable. I've always been told demons started the war but what if that's not the truth? What if we're the bad guys after all?

I don't know when I start crying but I can't make it stop. I press my face into the pillow, trying so hard to stifle the sounds so that Marcus won't hear them. It's humiliating. After everything that's happened so far, how can I lay here and *cry*? My internal chastising only makes it worse, but I do it anyway because I do believe I've lost my mind at this point.

Through the darkness, I risk a glance at my arm and the tattoo and think how drastically everything has changed in just a matter of hours. If Marcus hadn't risked his life to save mine, I'd be dead right now. If I somehow *had* managed to survive without him, I would've gone home as soon as I saw just how deep this whole thing goes, as soon as I realized how little I really know Ian.

I've left myself covered in scars yet I'll never know if you would've done the same for me.

"If you wanted a waterbed, you could've just asked," Marcus says suddenly.

"Huh?" I ask, sniffling suddenly in a pathetic attempt to gather myself. I have no idea how long he's been listening to me but it's most likely been long enough for the effort to hide the tears to be fruitless.

"Are you okay?" he asks.

"Great!" I say but my voice cracks and I hate myself again.

"What have I done to warrant a lie from you?" he asks, and I realize that he's moving closer.

"Nothing, it's just…" I don't know how to finish that sentence. I don't know how to explain the chaotic mess inside of me and I doubt I ever will. There's no way I can make him understand. Instead, the dam of my tears bursts again and the already soaking wet pillow takes the full brunt of the impact.

"Hey!" Marcus says, and I feel the edge of the bed dip as he sits down. He doesn't give me a chance to reply before he wraps his arms around me tightly. I'm rigid at first, but he doesn't let go, and I let myself dissolve into the contact. The first time a demon touched me without consequence I had just thought I was lucky, but now I know, demon skin really *doesn't* burn on contact—another lie I've been told by the Elders.

"You're not alone in this," he whispers in my ear and tries to pull away, but I hold firm. Now that he's so close, I suddenly don't care that he's a stranger. All I care about is the fact that he's right.

I don't know how long we stay like that, but I eventually manage to drift off to sleep with the feeling of drowning still very much in my head and chest. It feels so *peaceful* that I don't protest.

The next time I'm conscious, it's morning, and Marcus is still wrapped around me, his arm hanging loose as he snores into the pillow. As I study the delicate lines of his face, I'm amazed once again by my situation. I never thought I'd wake up in the same bed as a demon and feel nothing but warmth.

It's a cold day in Hell, I muse and rouse him from sleep.

"Huh? What?" Marcus asks, voice heavy with sleep as he reaches up to wipe a slick of drool off his chin.

"It's morning," I say simply and sit up.

He snorts to full consciousness as he realizes his arm is over my waist. He pulls it away but neither of us comment on it.

"I don't remember falling asleep," he admits and ruffles his dark hair.

"Me either," I reply and scoop my shoes up off the floor.

Marcus wrinkles his nose as he watches me.

"What?" I ask questioningly.

"Wouldn't you like to shower before heading back out?"

I shrug. "Why bother? The sooner we get going, the sooner the spell can be broken, right?"

Marcus sets his hand on my shoulder and I pause.

"You'll be better off changing outfits."

"Why?" I ask, raising my eyebrow.

"These are Old Demons we're supposed to be finding. If you think what regular demons did to you at the bar was bad, what do you think they'll do?"

A flash of Ian's body runs through my mind.

"Exactly," he says as if he's guessed my thoughts. "Go shower and wake up the rest of the way. I'll be back in a minute with a fresh change of clothes."

He doesn't listen to my protests so I do as he suggested.

I wait until I hear the sound of the door closing before I peek into the bathroom. It's immaculately clean, and the brightness of the white bothers me. It's *too* clean, like no one's ever been here before, but I know that's a lie. Whatever history the bathroom has, I'll never know.

That thought hits me hard when I step into the shower. The warm water feels good as it rinses away the layers of dirt and blood. I sigh and tilt my head backwards under the stream of water, letting it soak every lock of my hair, wiping away my own recent memories. The door to the hotel room creaks open suddenly and I freeze.

"Marcus?"

No response, but I can hear approaching footsteps passing through the tiny kitchen beyond the bathroom door. By the time I clean the water out of my eyes, the shower curtain is ripped aside, and I'm left staring an unfamiliar demon in the face.

13.

I SCREAM OUT and try to swipe at him, but he dodges and my foot slips on the slick bottom of the bathtub. I grab the curtain for support, but it tears from its frame easily under my weight, and I fall into the porcelain bowl, head smacking against the hard, white tiles. My vision swims as the demon smiles, staring down at me as if he's pleased that I'm already down and out without him having to do a thing to cause it.

He takes a step over the edge of the bathtub, smiling to show off sharp, broken teeth. I try to stand up, fingers clenching into the edge of the tub, but the surface beneath me is too slippery for me to get a grip. The slightest movement causes my head to spin, and before I know it, I'm back down again.

"Your kind disgusts me," the demon snarls, curling his lip to reveal even more broken teeth.

"The feeling…is mutual," I hiss back as soon as I catch a whiff of his breath.

Just then the door to the bathroom slams on its hinges, and Marcus rushes across the room. I blink, and in that second, the demon is thrown across the room to where he hits the sink and slips to the floor. A stream of red leaks from a wound on the side of his head, staining the sink and floor with the substance. When he lands on the floor, he props himself up on his elbows and looks down at the red puddle beneath him before looking back up at Marcus.

Marcus doesn't give him a chance to speak before he

kicks him in the face. Then he's on him, punching and punching until the demon is nothing but pulp and red liquid. I don't say anything for the longest time. I just sit crouched in the tub against the wall, hand held over my mouth and shower curtain clutched tight around me as I watch the display. When Marcus finally stops hitting the other demon, he is breathing so heavily I can see each rise and fall of his shoulders.

He doesn't turn to look at me as if he's forgotten I'm there. In this state, I'm almost terrified of catching his attention but a squeaking sound fills the room, and I realize it's *me*.

"Marcus," the squeaking noises finally say.

He turns to look at me, and I take in a sharp breath of air through my teeth when I catch sight of the blood splattered across his face. Marcus' eyes widen, and he lifts his arm, smearing half of the droplets onto the skin on his arm before he stands and crosses the room to me. I don't break eye contact as he drops to his knees by the edge of the tub.

"Talia, are you okay?" he asks at last then glances over his shoulder to the demon's remains. "He didn't hurt you, did he?"

I shake my head, but I still find it hard to speak. He reaches out his hand and tries to help me stand to my feet when he catches sight of a smear of blood on the wall where I had been sitting. He stops, and I do too, one leg inside the tub and one leg out, as I wait for him to speak.

"That's your blood," he says pointedly.

I bow my head, showing off the tender spot that had smashed into the wall. "I fell," I explain and feel his fingers prodding at the skin around the wound. I hiss through my teeth, and he pulls his hand back.

"Sorry," he says and leads me back into the room, helping me sit on the edge of the bed before he turns around to head toward the door.

"Where are you going?" I ask, eyes wide with fear. What if he decides this is enough? What if he leaves, and I'm stuck here, wounded, and in possession of a dead demon?

"Relax," he says, and I watch him scoop up a dress off the floor before he returns to my side. "I'm not going anywhere."

I put on the clothing, and Marcus helps me to dress the wound in my scalp. It's odd how long it actually takes for either of us to bring up the dead demon in the bathroom, but eventually it comes up again though my mind is so far gone, I can't recall if it was me or Marcus to actually ease it into the conversation.

"Who was he?" I find myself asking.

Marcus risks a glance toward the bathroom and runs a hand through his hair. "He's not one of the Old Demons, but…he's certainly older than most."

"He knew we were here," I say.

Marcus bobs his head. "No doubt. I wonder if some of these demons are more in tune with witches after their encounter with Shadow." He pauses to consider his own words. "Our buddy in the bathroom was most likely a scout."

I purse my lips. "A scout for what? Would they really send someone out to try and kill me? We're supposed to be helping them, aren't we?"

Marcus shrugs. "I have no idea what they're thinking or planning. I'm just telling you what I think."

I look at my hands in my lap. "Right."

"Either way," he says and rises to his feet, "I think we need to get the hell out of here before they realize he's not coming back and decide to come looking for him."

I nod, and that's the last words we say in the hotel room before we're back outside. I blink and narrow my eyes as they strain against the morning light. The place looks different in the sunlight, homier, like a place of wonder and possibilities rather than the darkness my coven had always told me existed on this side of the border.

We travel into the nearby line of trees without an ounce of hesitation, and I peer over my shoulder at the town we're leaving behind. "Shouldn't we stock up on some supplies before traveling out here?" I ask warily.

Marcus dips his shoulder down, and I catch sight of the strap of a backpack he has fastened there. In the haze of the intruder, I hadn't noticed he had one. "I already got you covered. We have enough food and water to last us a week."

"Will the trip take us that long?" I ask, feeling sicker with each footstep into the foliage we go. Here I had been concerned about a night when there's a good chance I might never return.

Marcus shakes his head. "I doubt it, but you never know."

I nod, glad for his "better safe than sorry" mentality. I tuck my hands into fists at my sides and fall into step behind Marcus. He's taller than me, and though I can't see the path ahead past him, I feel safer walking in his shadow, as if he can protect me simply by keeping me out of sight. That might be true for all I know.

The deeper into the woods we go, the colder it gets. Goosebumps raise up across my skin, and I fold my arms over my chest, desperate to preserve every ounce of warmth I can manage.

Marcus stops and pulls his backpack off before tugging out a sweater and tossing it to me. I gratefully accept, pulling the warm fabric over myself. "Why is it so cold here?" I dare myself to ask.

Marcus shrugs. "It's just the way they like it."

"I thought Hell was hot."

Marcus smiles. "Hell is all determined on perspective."

"Fair enough." It doesn't seem like much time passes before the chill breaches my newest layer of clothes, and I look at Marcus is envy. He's still wearing just a t-shirt, and I wonder how he manages it. For a little bit, I tell myself he's lying, that he's cold, but he doesn't want to seem weak in front of me, but his skin doesn't form goosebumps and he never shivers.

He really *isn't* cold and the thought both amuses and saddens me, and I don't understand myself. The way the sunlight peers through the trees casts Marcus into almost constant spotlights, and I can't take my eyes off of him. Demons are so similar to witches and so different. *Marcus* is so different from the way I've always pictured our rivals to look. He's beautiful in an unearthly way, and it took me until this moment to really realize that. My cheeks redden when he glances over his shoulder and catches my eyes on him.

He smiles and slows to match my pace. "You doing okay back here?"

I nod quickly and while the blush is on my face, I don't meet his gaze. "Yeah, I was just…thinking."

Amusement makes its way to his face. Is it possible that he knew what I had been thinking a moment sooner? "*About?*"

"How different demons and witches really are," I muse.

He shrugs as if it's the most obvious thing in the world. "Well, yeah. We're two different species. You wouldn't expect a cat and dog to be the same, would you?"

"It's different for us though. We're from the same ancestors, aren't we?"

"According to some people, but the fact that no one knows for sure means that anything is possible." There's a glint in his eyes when he says that.

For the rest of the day, I wonder what it means.

14.

WHEN THE SUN begins to fall, Marcus decides it's time for dinner. He passes me a bottle of water that I down almost instantly and a handful of various granola bars and fruit. I've never been much of a healthy eater, but in the moment, everything that touches my tongue tastes like pure bliss.

I pop the last bite of my granola bar in my mouth and wiggle against the rock I've been leaning on, hoping to find a better position to keep the wind off myself. Even Marcus finally gave into the cold and pulled on a sweatshirt. He downs a bottle of water but doesn't eat anything. I watch him questioningly.

"Don't you want to eat?" I ask at last.

He shrugs. "I don't think I can bring myself to do it."

I crumple the wrapper from my food in my first. "Nerves that bad?"

Marcus nods. "I've met the Old Demons once, when I was little, but from what I remember, they were terrifying."

That's something if it's coming from a demon.

"Is there anything *good* about these guys?"

Marcus blinks and looks at me. "If you gain their trust, they'll trust you fully for the rest of your life but getting to that point is so rare it barely ever happens."

"And for me that chance is even smaller," I say and blow a strand of hair from my eyes.

Marcus gives me an apologetic glance that I pretend I don't see. I don't have to be sorry for what I am, it's not something I had any say in. If the Old Demons don't like witches, they're entitled to their thoughts. I can think of plenty of witches—of all ages—who would rather chew off their own foot than be in the company of a demon for longer than five minutes.

"We should get going," I say and move to stand up but stop when I notice that Marcus isn't doing the same.

"Let's wait."

"What? It'll be dark soon."

"I know, that's what we're waiting for," he replies and rests the back of his head against the tree he's leaning on, staring up through the trees.

"Wait, but they might already see us as a threat. Wouldn't showing up in the dead of night make an even worse impression?" I ask, raising an eyebrow.

Marcus shakes his head. "The Old Demons prefer the darkness. Plus, it'll be easier for you to hide your face without the sunlight tattling on you."

I tilt my head to the side, considering his words. "That's a good point."

"I know," he says and smirks.

I laugh at his arrogance and cherish the feeling before the sound fades. Who knows the next time I'll be able to laugh again.

15.

WHEN WE FINALLY start to move again, it's well dark. So dark that I stopped being able to see and have clung to Marcus' arm for a majority of the trip for fear of falling over my own feet. If he minds, he doesn't say a word. I wonder how he can see with ease and find myself wondering if demons are capable of seeing in the dark. It would explain why the Old Demons prefer it. They have a technical advantage over their enemies.

Marcus starts to slow down, and I squint through the shadows, catching a foggy outline of a building up ahead. It reminds me of a church and the irony strikes me.

"We're close, aren't we?" I ask, trying to catch a glimpse of Marcus' profile in the dark.

He nods. "Yeah, just a few more minutes, and we'll be inside."

I purse my lips. "Are we supposed to just go inside?"

"As far as I know," Marcus says and begins to lead the way forward again. His body goes suddenly rigid, but I don't know if it's from the memories in his head or the task that we're about to embark on.

My senses are on full alert as we come to a door. I still can't see anything, but my mind is working full speed at guessing what's around me. I can almost *feel* the locations of the walls and objects around us even without being able to see them. As soon as we step inside the building, it feels as if we are surrounded with a crowd of demons, watching us and hissing their displeasure.

The way Marcus continues to walk on without slowing lets me know that it's all in my head. I try to shake the thoughts away, but they stay at the back of my mind, haunting me like an old lullaby.

"Are we alone here?" I ask finally.

"No," a voice speaks up.

It's not Marcus.

"What's the matter, little witch?" the voice seethes, and I clutch onto Marcus' arm, mind violently caught between fight or flight. "Are you afraid?"

Marcus wraps his arm around my shoulders as if he senses I'm about to bolt, and says, "We're not here as enemies."

"And how do *I* know that?" the voice hisses, and I feel a hand, cold as ice, caress my cheek.

Whimpering, I pull away, but in Marcus arms, I don't go very far.

"Because we were sent here to help," Marcus says, voice strong and once again, I find myself envying him.

The hand disappears from my face, and I feel the presence shift, most likely closing in on Marcus. His posture does not change. "We're here to help you get back a book?"

The thing hisses again and then silence. Somewhere in the distance, I can hear water dripping, and I look around, frantically trying to see where the beast went and why it's so quiet. A moment later, a dim light clicks on and even that proves to be too much. I squint, trying to see, but all I can make out is a blurry figure. I reach up to rub my eyes, and when I open them again, I see the figure is small, hunched over, and cloaked in a red robe, the hood so large that the shadow makes it impossible to see the wearer's face.

Marcus dips his head so that his eyes are on the floor and whispers for me to do the same. I comply though I'm not really sure why. They already know I'm a witch, don't they?

"Marcus," the voice hisses. It sounds ancient, the word a mere rasp from the hooded figure.

"Yes, sir," Marcus replies, still not looking up from the floor.

The hood shifts in my direction, and I know the figure is sizing me up. "You are a long way from home."

I don't say anything. I don't know what I *should* say. Would it be better to admit the truth or to try and lie?

Luckily, he doesn't wait for an answer. "You say you're here to help." It's not a question but rather a flat statement.

Marcus seems to interpret it as a question anyway. "Yes, sir. Reddick sent us."

"Ah," he says then glances at our arms, where the bind marks are visible. "And what of the witch?"

"It's a…long story," I force myself to say and then add an uncertain, "Sir."

"Reddick says there was a book that was stolen from you," Marcus says, sounding more like himself, and I peer at him from the corner of my eye.

The figure lets out a wheezing laugh, and the hood shifts in my direction again. Even though I can't see his face, I guess that he's looking at me in disgust simply by the previous noise he made. "Yes, one of our oldest in fact."

"We're here to get it back," I say.

"Well, little witch, that should be easy enough for you considering it's your kind who has current possession of it."

16.

MY BLOOD RUNS cold and I know without knowing that Ian has something to do with this.

"My kind? H-how do you know?"

The figure turns its head up just enough for me to see its mouth and the wicked smile that's etched there. "Your stench…you witches just don't realize how powerful it is."

I lift my arm to give an exaggerated sniff at my clothes, but I smell nothing. I press my lips into a tight line and avoid asking the one question I really want to know—what did the witch look like?

"How would a witch get in here to begin with?" Marcus asks. "The library is secure twenty-four seven, isn't it?"

"Yes, but all the guards in the world do not matter when you allow yourself to trust."

"You *trusted* a witch?" Marcus asks skeptically.

The figure smiles again. "As do you. They cast a spell over you and get inside your mind. When you're at your lowest, they strike."

"That's not true!" I blurt out and feel foolish for it. I have no idea *what* the witches who perpetrated this crime had done…Every day I'm learning more reasons to hate my own kind.

The figure says nothing to that. Instead, he takes slow step after slow step closer until he's about a foot away. My eyes are wide as I watch him, waiting to see what he'll do next. He's so close he could kill me with a single swipe of a hidden blade if he has the mind to do so and part of me is sure he does.

He leans closer and his acrid breath fills my nostrils until my eyes stream water. "You smell like him."

Marcus must sense how uncomfortable I am because he asks the one question I was too afraid to, "What did he look like?"

The demon looks at him and thankfully moves far enough away to ease my anxiety though when he answers Marcus' question, I feel sick all over again. I never really knew Ian at all.

I break into hysterics and the demon flinches backward as if he thinks I'm about to explode. "What's wrong with her?"

Marcus is silent, and I get it. If we say anything about knowing Ian this demon would see us as alliances and that would put us in hot water.

"P…panic attack," I force myself to say.

The demon does not move for the longest moment, and I fear that he won't believe me.

"She's under a lot of stress," Marcus says, pulling the demon's attention off of me again. "After all, you *did* send a demon after her this morning."

The figure cocks his head to the side. "No, child. We have done no such thing."

My mouth opens, and I have the desire to argue so strong on my tongue, but I don't know how to go about it. I know he's lying, he *has* to be, but how can I prove it?

"Not even to keep us from coming here in the case we might have sinister ideas for the rest of your books?"

"I can see your intentions better than you think. You'd

do best to not speak out of turn and remember that your Elders are your Elders for a reason, *child*," the Old Demon growls to Marcus.

Marcus and I send each other questioning glances. If these peddlers of black magic aren't responsible for my would-be assassin, then who is?

It's gotta be whoever killed Ian, I think.

Marcus pulls the side of his mouth up into an uncertain smile in an attempt to ease over the new tension. "Can you tell me a little bit about what was in the book that was stolen?"

The demon is statue-still again, refusing to move or to speak, and I assume he isn't going to answer Marcus' question because he's still too bitter about their tiny spat when he suddenly reaches up and pulls down his hood. His face is one crafted from the darkest of nightmares, and now, I'm having a *real* panic attack.

"It was the most important book in our possession."

"You said…one of the oldest?" I manage to say simply by avoiding looking at who I'm talking to.

"It was the origins of the riff between the witches and the demons. The history of our world and yours along with the ways of destroying us all."

"Why would you have a book like that?" Marcus asks, eyes wide. "That's just asking for trouble."

"What are we without history? If there was no record of our origins, who would remember where we've been, where we've come from? Who will keep us from making the same mistakes again and again and again?"

"You're sure a witch took it?" I ask softly.

"I am never wrong," he says and fixes me with a look through his half-decayed eyes that rolls my stomach.

"We believe you," Marcus says.

The demon dips his head. "Now that you know the importance of the mission ahead of you, do you still wish to offer us your assistance?"

Considering our situation, I'm stunned by the question. This demon is no doubt powerful, and instead of ordering us to do his bidding, he's giving us a choice. Even Reddick hadn't done that.

Things are very strange indeed.

Marcus looks at me, and I look right back at him. "Yes, we do."

"Follow me," the demon says and pulls his hood back up.

Of course I don't want to do that. I want to go the opposite way through the door outside and keep going all the way back through last night, back to when I had been an ignorant witch pining for her lost love. But I can't. It seems like such a long time ago now that it's almost hard to believe it had ever been real.

My head is bowed as I follow behind Marcus. He looks around, studying the architecture of the next room we enter, but I only look up long enough to ensure I'm not going to crash into anything. That single glance tells me that this new room is a library complete with ceiling-high bookshelves stacked with books. I risk another glimpse up, marveling in awe. I wonder how they can tell just one is missing in a room this large.

"Our library has some of the oldest books in the world," the demon says as we go deeper into the room.

Marcus looks around, but he doesn't seem as impressed as I am. He doesn't speak as we come to the end of the library. On this wall is a hanging bookshelf that covers ninety percent of it but under the lip where it ends is a door. At first, I almost don't see it but then the demon reaches out and sets his bone white hand on the golden doorknob.

"The most important books stay in here," he says and reaches into the folds of his robes to pull out a single key.

The door opens with ease and inside, the room is pitch black until the demon takes one step inside then it's illuminated with light. Every wall in this room is covered in shelves with books, all of which are covered with a series of intricate bars and locks.

"So, you *really* trusted him," Marcus says at last after we have a moment to survey the room.

"Yes, and he used that trust to stab us in the back."

I know the feeling, I think and drop my gaze once again to the floor. "You said a witch has it?"

The demon nods. "No one on this side of the border has it any longer."

"And how do you know that for sure?" Marcus asks.

"Call it a gut feeling, if you will," the demon muses and crosses the room. He sets his hand over the bars but the space behind it is empty.

17.

WE LEAVE LESS than five minutes later, and I don't feel good about the information that I've learned.

"If Shadow stole the book from them, who stole it from Shadow?" Marcus asks the same question I have in my mind.

"I don't know," I say, and my lip trembles. Whoever stole the book from him didn't just take the book, they took his life as well.

"Whatever happened, the end story is a witch has it now," Marcus says and runs his hand through his hair. "Any ideas on who that could be?"

I shake my head. "All we can do now is cross the border and investigate."

Marcus freezes instantly. "You want me to travel to *your* side of the border?"

I stop and turn to look at him, narrowing my eyes to try and gauge his emotion. "Well, yeah. If you want to help me get the book and break this bind then you don't really have a choice, do you?"

Marcus looks down at the ground and breathes out slowly.

I take a small step toward him. "Hey, are you okay?"

He looks up at me through his lashes. "Honestly? I've never crossed the border before, I don't know…what to expect on the other side."

I blink and don't know how to reply to that. I want to

tell him that he'll be okay, that no one will harm him, that *they* are good people like he reassured me his townsfolk were, but all of those feel like lies. The truth is, I don't want to cross the border either. I know Abigail is still waiting on the other side to burden me with questions the second I return.

Or maybe she took up her threat of telling the Elders where I've been, who knows?

"I wish there was something I could say to make you feel better," I admit.

He smirks. "Your people are really that bad, are they?"

I shrug. "They're not who I used to think they were."

He must hear the pain in my voice because he doesn't push the topic further. Instead, he reaches down and takes my hand in his.

"We've got this."

18.

T HE WAY BACK to the border is long and exhausting. For fear of being seen after the incident with the demon in the hotel room, we make a camp in the woods that night, and continue our journey in the morning. Marcus has a bit more pep in his movements, and I want to believe the sun is to thank for it. When the creek finally comes into view—the invisible boundary line with it—I glance up at him.

His face is stoic, eyes fixed firmly on the small stream of water. "It's so innocent, isn't it? A creek. Like it doesn't separate two bodies of evil from one another, it's crazy."

"It is," I say and hop over it with ease. I glance back over my shoulder to see him still standing rigid on the other side. "What's the matter?"

"Demons can't cross running water," he explains, looking back up at me before tilting his head slightly. "Witches aren't supposed to be able to either."

"I'm not a full-blooded witch," I answer. "Ian wasn't either. Both of us had one human parent."

"Huh, okay. The more you know," he says and shrugs then looks down at the water again. "What do I do?"

"I've got an idea," I say and pick up a couple heavy stones, tossing them into the creek to break up the flow of water. "What about that?"

"Won't know if I don't try," he replies and takes a step forward.

I clench my hands into fists as I watch him navigate and

less than a moment later, he's made it.

"See? That wasn't so bad," I say.

"Says you," he grunts, fingers digging into the dirt as he looks up at me through his black bangs.

"At least you made it." I shrug and cross to the creek, plucking the stepping stones out of the water before flinging them onto the shore a few feet away.

Marcus shoots me a questioning glance.

"We don't want just anyone crossing, right?" I explain.

He sits up on his knees and looks around. "It doesn't seem much different on this side."

"Why would it?" I ask as if I hadn't had the exact same thought two nights ago when *I* crossed the border for the first time.

"Don't know," Marcus says and stands to his feet, wiping away the leaves and dirt from his knees before he looks down at me. "Okay, this is your land. Where do we go?"

I sigh. "I have no idea. I guess the first thing is to see how far we get."

"Expecting company?" he asks.

"Depends on if Abigail was true to her word."

Marcus scoffs. "Witches." A pause. "So, I don't think you've told me where we're going."

I glance at him over my shoulder, a weird gesture in itself. This entire trip, I've been trailing him like a lost puppy, and now it's his turn to assume the role.

"I don't know about you, but I could use a change of clothes and a hot meal," I say.

"I get to see your house, eh?" he asks.

"Yeah, but before you ask, no. it's not glamorous."

He shrugs. "Perspective is entirely dependent on the individual, isn't it?"

"Fair enough," I pout, feeling all the fight leave me.

My feet tread the familiar path with ease and when we make it to my house, I just stare. It's hard to believe it's been *days* since the last time I've seen my own front door.

An irritated meow sounds from the shadows behind the hedges that surround the house. A mottled cat emerges, ears flat to her head in annoyance.

"Mushroom, I'm so sorry!" I say, kneeling beside her. "You must be starving."

The cat bows her head then her gaze flicks to Marcus, and she freezes. Her hackles raise one hair at a time, and she lets out a sharp hiss. I put a hand on her head, and the hiss stops like she's nothing more than a furry alarm clock.

"I'm sorry," I say to Marcus and open the door.

Mushroom pads inside the open door, but Marcus stays in place, peering after her warily. "Uh, that cat isn't going to attack me, is it?"

I shake my head. "She's not a cat. Mushroom is my familiar. She's actually really pleasant, she just gets crabby when she's hungry."

"I'll take your word for it," Marcus says and takes one step forward before he pauses again. "Wait, familiar? As in she's half human?"

I nod. "Yeah, but she prefers to stay in her cat form. She won't be any trouble for us."

He doesn't argue again as I plod into the kitchen and pull a steak out of the fridge. I put it on a plate and set it on the floor. Mushroom purrs her approval and bounds forward, tearing into the food.

"She really *was* hungry," Marcus says, watching the tiny beast in all of her ferocity. "Will she tell I'm here?"

I shake my head. "Her loyalty is pledged to me so I doubt it. I mean she won't even eat without my okay, but even saying that, I can't guarantee anything. She is a free being with a mind of her own so who knows."

Marcus leans his elbows on the kitchen island and glances around. "This place is cozy."

Mushroom looks up and a gob of food falls from her mouth. She meows once, and Marcus freezes as if he assumes the cat is about to lunge at him for speaking.

"She agrees," I translate, and Mushroom resumes her meal. "Come on," I say to Marcus.

I lead the way out of the kitchen and down the hall to my room. Marcus is uncharacteristically silent as he looks around again.

"If you want a change of clothes, I have some old outfits of Ian's in the closet." I can't even bring myself to look at the door.

Marcus gets up and crosses the room so I distract myself by ruffling through my dresser in search of one of my baggy, comfortable dresses when I hear the closet swish open.

A moment later, Marcus says, "You really cared about him."

My hands clutch around the shirt I had been holding. "Yeah." That one word has all the strength in the world to break me down.

At the sound of my tears, Marcus is quick to react just like he had been the last time. He gathers me in his arms, and I cry into his chest, not even noticing the natural odor that comes from a male going three days without a shower.

He strokes my hair, and I glance up at him, tears still in my eyes. Then he kisses me. His lips are soft and gentle as they press against mine, and the next I know, we're lying in my bed. He leaves a trail of kisses down my neck, and I snake my hand up into his hair. When he meets my eyes, he freezes, as if he thinks he's made some kind of mistake, but he hasn't. I don't want him to stop. I've only ever been with Ian, and I want the memory to fall far out of my head.

I pull Marcus back to me and press my lips to his as my fingers tug at the bottom of his shirt.

"Talia, are you sure you—"

"Shh," I say, and I urge him to sit up just enough to slip off his shirt before I move to kissing his neck.

He lets out the slightest moan, and I smile at the sound before I lift a hand to trace the band of his jeans. The skin on his stomach is warm, taut. The abs quiver under my touch, and I take that as my cue to move forward. Not at all subtly, I shove my hand into his pants. He's already hard, and I grasp at the base of his penis, letting my fingers run its length to the tip. He shivers in delight and looks down at me through eyes narrowed with lust.

"Did you really like this dress?" he whispers huskily into

my ear.

I shake my head, and the tearing of fabric as he rips it from my body fills the room. I shiver as the cool air breezes across my bare flesh, causing my nipples to harden. Marcus sits back on his knees, admiring me as he undoes the buttons and zipper of his jeans.

My breathing deepens as he pulls them down his thighs, revealing everything to me. His jeans land on the floor next to my battered dress and he lunges forward, kissing me again. One finger trails from my collarbone, over my left breast, across my stomach, and into the wetness between my legs.

I let out a soft moan, and my hands claw into his back. He flexes under my fingers, working his finger inside of me. He nibbles my bottom lip before he pulls his finger out of me and holds it up for me to see.

He puts it in his mouth, wiping away all traces of me with his tongue. "You taste amazing, witchy," he says, and I feel his member press against my stomach before he readjusts and the tip prods at my entrance. He pauses then, and I groan.

"You're *sure* you want to do this?" he asks.

I buck my hips in response, taking more of his penis inside of me, until he gives up on the question and plunges himself the rest of the way inside. He thrusts faster and harder, panting in my ear as I writhe and moan beneath him, rising slowly to climax until I feel him orgasm, a burst of warmth inside of me, and I join him in ecstasy less than a second later.

Marcus gathers me in his arms and kisses me on the forehead but neither of us speaks. In the aftermath of what we had just done, it seems almost *too* quiet.

"Is it okay if I take a cat nap?" he asks at last, peeking at me with a small playful smile on his face. "No Mushroom included."

"That's fine," I say and smile back.

I sit up, wrapping myself in the sheet as I sit on the edge of the bed, suddenly self-conscious.

"Where are you going?" Marcus asks and by the sound of his voice, I can tell he's already well on his way to falling asleep.

"I'm gonna get something to eat," I reply, but he's already snoring.

I sigh and get up, pulling on a sweater and pair of leggings before I drop the sheet to the floor and trudge out to the kitchen. Mushroom, still in her cat form, is sitting on the kitchen island. As soon as I step foot into the kitchen, she tilts her head to the side in her classic way of saying, "You have some explaining to do."

I fold my arms across my chest as her gaze settles on me. "He's a friend."

The head tilt intensifies.

I sigh. "Okay, I don't know *what* he is now. I met him three nights ago when…when I crossed the border."

Mushroom's eyes go wide, and she holds up her tail— her way of telling me to wait a moment—before she disappears from the room. When she reappears, she's in her human form, cloaked in a simple white dress. She is painfully beautiful to look at with her golden blonde hair and rosebud lips. Whenever I see her like this, I wonder why she hates it so much.

Humans...lie to others, to people like me. As a cat, I can see who they are inside, *without their intentions getting in the way,* she had said once.

Mushroom folds her arms across her chest to mimic me. "Now, you were saying?"

"I crossed the border the other night."

Her mouth falls open. "You didn't!"

I nod and hold out my tattooed arm. "I wish I could say that."

"What is that?" she asks, tapping her slender finger to my skin.

"A binding spell," I reply and poke at it as well.

Mushroom glares toward the bedroom, fire in her eyes. "Did *he* do that to you?"

"In a way," I muse, and when the fire in her intensifies, I add, "He saved my life."

"How?"

"I tried to figure out where Ian had been on the night he died, and well, it led me eventually to this underground black magic shop. Marcus showed me the way, and when the dealer all but killed me, he made the deal to save my life."

"*He's* Marcus, right?" she asks for clarification.

I nod. "We can't break the bond until we get back what Ian stole."

Mushroom cocks an eyebrow. "So, he was the bad guy in this whole thing?"

"It gets worse," I say and lean against the counter. "The Old Demon we talked to says that the book contained secrets of how to permanently kill demons and witches…not to mention a variety of other things."

"The book wasn't with him when he died?" she asks.

"No. Whoever killed him took it."

Mushroom purses her lips. "It's gotta be another witch."

"Marcus thinks so too, but I don't know who it could be. Who would kill Ian, and if it is another witch, *why* would they do it?"

"They wanted the book. To me, it seems as if Ian didn't work alone. Maybe him and another witch had a plan, but Ian had second thoughts and the other witch killed him to keep him from taking the book away. Have you considered the idea of a partner? Someone equally able to cross the border with minimal to no detection?"

My mouth hangs open. Everything is so clear to me now that it hurts that I haven't connected the dots sooner. "Abigail," I breathe.

Mushroom tilts her head.

"It's Abigail! It has to be her," I say and touch Mushroom's shoulder. "The first night I was in the demon's territory, she came looking for me *over* the border. I never knew she could cross but…"

"There's your answer," Mushroom concedes, her amber eyes boring into mine.

As if an answer from the Gods above, the doorbell rings.

19.

USHROOM'S EYES ARE too big again. I blink, and that's all the time it takes for her to return to her cat form. She jumps up onto the sink, peering out the window to catch a glimpse of whoever it is on the porch. Her ears flatten nearly instantly, and my blood runs cold.

The Council of Elders, alerted by Abigail most likely. Mushroom nearly flies off the sink, and I scoop her up into my arms before running into the bedroom to shake Marcus awake.

"Marcus! Marcus! We have to go!" I say, throwing his clothes at him one by one.

"Wha-why?" he asks through his daze of sleep.

"The Elders are here. If they see you, they'll kill us both. We have to get out of here."

That bolts him awake, and he throws his clothes on with too much precision for the speed he moves and slings his bag over his shoulder as I half-drag him toward the bathroom window. I encourage him to go first, and I pass him Mushroom—to which he's too shocked to comment on—before I finally pull myself through.

We dash into the woods just beyond the perimeter of my house as the sound of the door being kicked in rings out into the silence. I don't look back again as we dash through the trees.

"Where do we go?" Marcus asks frantically, and I notice Mushroom is still in his hands. She jumps free then and bolts into the woods.

"Only one place to go," I reply and begin to follow her.

"Abigail's!"

"Why? She can't help us. Need I remind you of her threat?"

"She's the one, Marcus," I say. "The one who stole the book, the one who killed Ian. It's been her the entire time.

"Witchy, you have no luck for friendship."

"I really don't."

A minute later, I'm convinced we've gotten a good enough lead to afford to take some time to breathe. Mushroom's tail wags anxiously as she looks around, sniffing the air. I wait until the redness fades from Marcus' face before I continue onward once again, letting my anger take control of me this time. When I reach Abby's house, I don't bother to knock, but instead, I kick the door in.

Her home opens into her kitchen, and she's seated at her dining room table as if she had been waiting for us, but at the sound of the door, she leaps to her feet. Her familiar, an orange tabby named Chase, bolts for cover.

"You," I say.

Abigail's eyes are still wide as she makes an attempt to regain herself.

"You killed him," I say. "And it was you who sent that demon to try to kill me, wasn't it? How *could* you? I thought you were my friend!"

Her shock fades away quickly, *too* quickly as if it had never been genuine. "The power he had? It really goes to someone's head, you know? The boy couldn't make rational decisions on his own anymore." She shrugs. "I did him a kindness."

"And what did I ever do? Huh? Was my friendship such a burden you felt the need to eliminate me?"

"No idea what you're talking about, my dear. Witches die on demon territory all the time," she says and smiles, a bright twinkle in her eye.

"You think I'm stupid, don't you? I can see it in your eyes, *hear* it in your tone. When your lips curve into that little half-smirk, I just want to split your face. It shows off the bitch in you too well."

"Oh, honey, don't you get it? Ian would've done *anything* for me, including die." She tips her head back to laugh, and I stand rigid in place.

"I get it too well. I'm smarter than anyone thinks, but I guess it doesn't matter now, does it? I always liked you for your independence, but I just realized you don't have any. You…dabbled with black magic because it was taboo, right? Because the Elders said it was forbidden like so many teenagers before you. Well, that's the problem with sheep. They follow."

She holds a hand over her heart, pretending to be hurt by my words. "You can throw some *knives*, Tally! But you know, for all the names you're calling me, it doesn't matter. Ian saw something in me. Something he never saw you in. He was always super creative in the bedroom, especially when it came to names, but I don't need to tell you that. You know for yourself just how wonderful of a lover he could be."

My vision flashes red, and I can't stop my body from reacting to it. I lunge forward, Marcus' cries for me to stop somewhere in the background, but not near enough for me to make sense of them or care.

Abigail laughs again, her eyes flashing ruby red as she throws out her hand, releasing a blast of energy that sends me flying against the wall. "Aww, sweetie. Are you mad that I took your boy toy away?"

I gnash my teeth to try and ignore the pain that's biting at me from my left arm, my shoulder, and the back of my head where the impact had been the greatest. "I'll kill you."

"Will you?" she asks and closes the extended hand into a first. My guts feel as if they're turning to liquid.

I try to move to stop her, but my arms are stuck against the wall like shackles, and I know that wherever Chase is hiding, he's responsible.

"I've learned a lot about witches and demons this week. A lot about what good and evil really means. Today's the day you'll learn the same, and finally see for yourself that in the end, goodness *always* wins."

"God, don't you ever stop talking?" Abigail asks sarcastically. "You always drive me crazy with that shit. It's like, just close your mouth. No one wants to hear your speeches, no one cares what you're *thinking*, and I just…" She holds her hand up to her head and swipes at her eyebrow before looking down at me again, her eyes blazing as red as the ruby around her neck. "No one *cares.*" The pain inside of me intensifies. It's as if someone's taken a blender to my stomach, my intestines, and my ribs and all I can think about is how much I want to die.

"I was…only your friend…because I felt…s-sorry for you," I rasp, sneering at her even through the pain. "Everyone else…hates you…th-that's why you turned…where you did. If peop…people didn't love you by choice…you'd *force* them to. Y-you did it to Ian. He never…would've gave a damn about you…otherwise."

Her heavy red lips turn up into such a sharp smile that I'm sure it has to hurt. "That's where you're *wrong,* I'm happy to say! He's the one person I *didn't* have to enchant."

"I…don't believe you. I won't," I snarl, pressing my hand into the pain in my stomach to keep my focus on my ex-friend rather than the rising tide of nausea in my stomach.

"The truth is always so bitter. That's why you just gotta swallow it down. Besides, didn't your Mama ever tell you to never lose your head over a boy?" Abigail sneers. "After all, he wasn't *everything* you made him out to be. He was actually quite stupid, trying to pull one over on *me?* That was just no bueno."

I glare at her, a bit of blood running from my mouth to drip onto the floor as the information processes.

"That bastard actually thought he could slip out into the night, and I would never notice anything was amiss, but that book was everything. He just didn't understand that by doing what he did, he put me in the position to choose, and it was never really a choice to begin with. He was a means to an end. So, I stabbed him in the neck and took back what was mine."

The rage comes in a swell of blinding grief, and I try to lunge again, but I can't move. Chase's magic is too strong so I resort back to words instead. "He turned on you…because the spell wore off, and he realized…he'd rather die than be with an arrogant, stuck up, wannabe—" Another blinding flash of pain erupts in my stomach and as much as I want to finish that sentence, I can't. I find it difficult just to breathe.

Abigail is all smiles again as she watches every second of my suffering, and I stare right back at her, hoping the Devil has a room specifically crafted for her in Hell. Then her gaze falls off of me and instead focuses on Marcus.

"I wonder how compliant this pet will be," she says, taking a slow step forward. "You know, for a demon, he's really not that bad looking. With some work, he could be truly beautiful, like a statue. Imagine how good he would look with me. It takes so little these days to win a man's heart. Just one kiss, and he'll be mine."

Marcus' face twists at those words, but he hasn't been able to move the entire time that I've been immobilized. For the most part, his face has been impassive but as soon as he realizes the danger has turned to him, he's desperate to free himself though he knows as well as I do that all the struggling in the world can't break through magic like this.

"You better not touch me, witch," he growls through bared teeth.

"Or what?" Abigail asks, tipping her head to the side so that her ridiculous pigtails fall sideways. "Seems you'd do better if you begged for my mercy."

Marcus scoffs. "That right? Well, I'd rather die than grovel to a witch, especially one as repugnant as you."

"Well, what exactly can you do when you can't move?" Abigail's face is venomous, then, in a split second, everything changes.

She gasps horribly, her anger snubbing out as her face twists in an unforgettable mask of pure horror. She holds a hand up over her heart and a torrent of red begins to slip through the gaps in her fingers before she falls to her knees, revealing Mushroom standing behind her.

"Nothing at all, bitch," she says.

20.

"MUSHROOM!" I GASP and spit out another gob of blood onto the dark floor. "Her familiar…"

"On it," she replies and pulls her knife free from Abigail's gasping, bleeding body, before she ducks into the shadows under the brim of the tablecloth.

Horrific cat-like screeches ensue, and she emerges a moment later, blood covered hand grasping the orange tabby by the nape of the neck.

"What do you say?" she taunts Chase.

He looks punitive as he glares back at her.

She tightens her grip, shaking him slightly. He growls and then just like that, the magic is lifted. I gasp, glad to be able to draw in large mouthfuls of air again, and hold a hand to my throat on reflex. Marcus does the same before he rushes over to me, pulling me into his arms. He looks over the bruises on my arm before he asks, "Are you okay?"

I nod and look at Mushroom who is still holding Chase as condescendingly as possible. "Who's a cute little pussy cat?" she's singing to him.

I laugh and let Marcus help me stand to my feet before I walk over to her and pull Mushroom into my arms. "You are the best familiar ever."

"Why didn't his magic work on you?" Marcus asks Mushroom, glaring at the tabby in her hand.

"Silly, familiar magic doesn't affect other familiars."

"Thank God for that," I say and set my hand on her shoulder. "You, my dear, are a Godsend."

She smiles and kisses me on the cheek before her attention returns to Chase. "What do we do with him?"

"Keep him in a nice small pet carrier. He's our star witness," I say.

Chase only growls.

In the distance, I hear the sound of movement and know that it's the Elders closing in on us. I lift my hands slowly into the air, and Marcus does the same, a moment before the Council appears in Abigail's open door.

21.

"SO, YOU SEE, your Honor, we are not to blame for Abigail's death," I say, holding my chained hands before me. "It was self-defense."

The Head of the Elders pulls her tiny spectacles off her face and uses her thumb and index fingers to pinch her eyes as she rests her elbows on the table.

"Miss Gram, do you really expect us to believe such a wild tale? If it is true, you have conspired with a demon and slain a fellow witch."

I send a small glance over my shoulder to the table where Marcus and Mushroom sit side by side, heavy chains bound around their wrists as well. "Abigail was not who we thought she was. She killed Ian. She tried to kill me. I think she wanted to use black magic to take over our Coven."

"This is all heresy and speculation," a different member of the Council says.

"Perhaps," I reply, "but Miss, we have a witness."

Mushroom lifts the cat carrier off the floor and sets it on the table. Chase's amber eyes gleam out from the shadows.

"Ask him anything you wish, for as you know, a familiar cannot lie to a witch."

It only takes about five minutes for the Elders to pull all of the truth out of Chase. The Head made him change into his human form before the questioning begun, and it's almost embarrassing; he's a mess of tears and ugly sobbing by the time the entire thing comes to an end. The Head waves her wrist, and Chase is taken away to the prison chambers by two witches to await his punishment. Then, her hawk-like gaze falls onto us.

"Well, it seems as if you have committed no crime, but were just unfortunate enough to be caught up in something much larger than yourself. While I am not thrilled of the idea of a demon being here on this side of the land, seeing as how you were charged to stop something that could've been detrimental to us all, I will look the other way just this once."

I hold my breath, clasping my chained hands over my heart.

"Mushroom, Talia, while I do not hold any ill will against you, breeching the boundary set forth by our ancestors is a serious offense. Hereby, I sentence you to banishment. You have until tonight, then you must be gone from our Coven. If there is a glimpse of you spotted when the sun rises tomorrow morning, you will be eligible for execution. Meeting dismissed."

I'm frozen as the witches hover around me, undoing my chains, as well as those bound to Mushroom and Marcus. We're escorted from the room, but none of us speak until we're pushed outside and left alone to stare at one another in the dark.

"Banished," Mushroom says and runs her tongue along her lip. "Imagine that."

"It's better than whatever Chase is going to get," I remind her. "At the very least, we're free."

"You're not upset?" Marcus asks, surprise in his voice as he looks down at me.

I shake my head. "I've always kind of hated it here. Ian

was the only one who ever made it feel worthwhile, and he…he was never right for me. I can't wait to get out of here."

"Where will you go?" Marcus asks.

I freeze at the coldness of the question. For some reason, I had assumed he would invite me with him. After all, the book still needs to be returned to Reddick for the curse to be broken, but he could do that part alone, couldn't he?

"I…I don't know," I finally say and look at the ground, feeling the slight sting of rejection.

"Hey, don't look like that. The reason I'm asking is I'm not going home either."

I scrunch my face, intrigued by his words. "But why? You haven't been banished."

"No, but there's just nothing left for me there. Pickpocketing drunk girls and occasionally dabbling in black magic? That's not much of a life, even for a demon. Besides, I'm sure they found the demon I killed."

I purse my lips. "So, what do you suggest?"

"Isn't it obvious, silly?" Mushroom pipes up. "He's saying we should start over somewhere new."

Marcus sends her a crooked smile. "Exactly. It'll be just like in the old days when witches and demons got along before the war ever came to be." He extends his hand to me. "What do you say?"

I set my hand on his open palm. "That sounds like a wonderful idea."

"But first the book," Mushroom reminds us.

My shoulders droop. "Abigail never did tell us where she hid it."

"No matter, her little kitty sang like a canary for me. Pardon the irony."

Marcus and I exchange mischievous smiles as Mushroom changes back into her cat form and disappears into the trees a second after flashing a signal in tail twists and bends.

"She says, 'Be back in a minute,' " I translate.

Marcus laughs, and I look at him. "What?"

"It's just crazy that you can *understand* her while she's a cat."

I shrug and watch her disappear. "In time you'll learn to speak all things Mushroom."

"That'll be the day," he says, and Mushroom emerges from the foliage once again.

She's in her human form this time and holds a beaten leather-bound book out to me. "Ta-da."

"That's the best magic in the world," I reply and take the book from her.

"Where was it hidden?" Marcus asks. "You were gone for like, fifteen seconds."

"Under a rock," Mushroom says brightly and laughs. "Abigail wasn't as smart as she thought she was."

I laugh with her as my eyes drop to the book again. It's far heavier than it should be, but it's not a physical weight I feel. This book not only contains the entire history of the demon and witch races, it was also the reason behind Ian's death…and it killed me too, in a way.

I would be such a different person if Ian was still alive.

That thought is jolting.

22.

WE GO BACK to my house and gather essentials like food, clothes, and blankets. I take nothing of sentimental value because nearly everything I own reminds me of Ian in some shape or form. Where I'm going, I don't want to be reminded of what I can't change. It's strange to look around and think it'll be the last time I'll see this place I've come to call home, but the thought is hardly a whisper, and surprisingly, easy to ignore.

Mushroom resumes her cat form and spends the beginning of the journey draped across my shoulders—her reward for a job well done. Marcus stays by my side the entire time, never straying ahead or falling behind. When we hit the border, I stand there for a moment, just staring back across the land—and life—that I'm leaving behind.

"Will you miss it?" Marcus asks.

I stare for a moment longer before I tear my gaze away. "Not like I thought I would."

He smiles and sets his hand on my shoulder, gently guiding me deeper into his land and away from this place in which I am to never return. Mushroom swipes her paw across my collarbone, and I know that's her way of offering me her comfort. I tap her paw, stroking the fur gently, before releasing her.

"Don't tell me if I'm wrong…but you already seem happier, witchy," Marcus says.

I reply with a smile. "I'm just lost in thought."

"Good thoughts I hope."

The last time I had walked this path, I had had no idea of what to expect. Even though things are up in the air right now, I feel as if I have real control over my life that I've never had before. We don't take the exact same route, of course. We make sure to take a wide circle around the bar since we have no idea whether or not the mob will still be searching for us. When we pass the alley that had led to Marcus' home, I stop and look at him.

"Don't you want to see your house one last time?" I ask.

He shakes his head and keeps walking with barely a second of thought. "The last time was enough for me."

I follow his lead and subconsciously, we resume our leader-and-lost-puppy-form of travel. I'm still admittedly frightened of Reddick and with Mushroom draped across my shoulders, I'm afraid for me *and* her. After all, I have no idea how demons even feel about familiars.

Marcus must sense the change in my emotions because he encourages me to stay in his shadows as we head inside the creepy building cloaked in darkness.

Reddick is standing by the door as if he knew we would appear. As we emerge side by side, he smiles at us both like we're at a high school reunion. "It feels as if it's been years since I've seen your smiling faces!"

His gaze turns to me, and I realize he's looking at Mushroom. "Well, furball, I don't believe we've met."

"We have the book," I say, dropping to my knees before Reddick can focus any more attention on Mushroom. She skitters to the floor and hides in the shadows behind Marcus' legs as I open my backpack and pull out the book like it's a giant gem. It is, in a way.

Reddick's eyes glow with delight as he takes it from me. "This is it all right." Reddick opens his jacket, and I see a long, curved knife strapped on the inside. On the other side, it's blank but there's a pocket there that Reddick sticks the book into.

I glance to Marcus wondering if it was really for the best to give a dabbler of black magic a book filled with secrets of the world, but for some reason it feels right. I know that he's close to the Old Demons and there's a feeling in my gut that assures me it'll find its way back to the library.

"You, come here," Reddick says to Marcus as I work on tying my backpack shut.

Marcus nods and lets his fingers dance across the top of my head before he complies. Mushroom, exposed to Reddick's line of sight once again, skitters behind me to hide, crouching down to make herself look smaller than I've ever seen her.

"Can't you make yourself into a kitten so you can be even easier to hide?" I whisper to her.

She blinks but doesn't look amused by the question.

I glance toward Reddick and Marcus as they stand face to face, staring one another down. Reddick reaches out, setting his hand on Marcus' right shoulder. "This will hurt," he informs him then glances past Marcus to me as I stand up off the floor. "For both of you."

He grabs Marcus' left arm, and we both scream out. I drop back to my knees again and look up at Marcus who is still on his feet. I imagine that without Reddick to hold him up, he would most likely be on the ground as well. The pain deepens and a white light blasts out from my arm, matching the light coming out of Marcus. When Reddick finally lets go, the light and pain fades away and the tattoos are gone.

Reddick, with the book tucked against his breast, is surprisingly pleasant and wishes us safe travels before he disappears into the depths of his home.

We watch for the better part of a minute. "I can't tell if we made a friend of him or if he's still an enemy," I muse at last.

Marcus laughs. "Same here."

I scoop up Mushroom, and we leave the old shack, wandering out into the night with laughter in our throats, and hope in our hearts.

About the Author

Kayla Frederick is the new pen name for established author, Kayla Krantz. A little neurotic and a huge lover of Halloween, she enjoys creepy stories.

www.ingramcontent.com/pod-product-compliance
Lightning Source LLC
Chambersburg PA
CBHW030807190726
48285CB00003B/1065